THE NAVY OF HUMANKIND: WASP SQUADRON

BOOK 5

INDOMITABLE

Colonel Jonathan P. Brazee
USMC (Ret)

Acknowledgements:

I want to thank all those who took the time to offer advice as I wrote this book. A special shout-out goes to real Navy air warrior, CAPT Andres Brugal, USN (Ret.) for keeping helping me with "air-speak" and culture, and to my beta readers James Caplan, Kelly O'Donnell, Micky Cocker, and Jim McNeill for their valuable input

Cover by Jude Beers

DEDICATION

Captain Hilliard Wilbanks, United States Air Force

OV-1 Reconnaissance Pilot

KIA 24 February, 1967

Awarded the Medal of Honor

Lieutenant Colonel Hugh Mills, United States Army (Ret)

OH-6 Scout Pilot

Awarded the Distinguished Flying Cross

DEEP SPACE, SECTOR GR-141

Chapter 1

"Got you, sucka!" Naval Enlisted Pilot First Class Floribeth Salinas O'Shea Dalisay, callsign "Fire Ant," said as she eased off her bow thrusters and slid in behind the FAL.

The Crystal had made a break for it as the rest of the squadron tightened the noose, but Fox Flight, playing the angel role, had swooped in for the kill.

"Damn, you get all the luck, sista!" Mercy Dalisay, her sister-in-law and wingman, passed over the S2S. "Like always."

"Can't help it if they come my way," Beth said.

Which was an understatement. Fox Flight was referred to as the "honey flight." It seemed that in every fight, Fox was in the thick of things, attracting FALs, no matter what mission the CO assigned to them.

If Fox Flight was the "honey-flight," Beth herself was the "FAL-magnet." She was the first human to have run into "Fucking Aliens," as Navy personnel called the crystalline enemy, back when she was a commercial scout pilot, and that propensity for contact had never ceased.

Beth watched her probability of success reach forty-two percent. Her firing AI only dealt with cold, hard facts. It was not programmed to consider intuition, but Beth sure could, and she knew that her POS would rise given a bit more time.

The CO was not a fan of intuition, but the CO didn't have twelve confirmed kills, the most of any pilot in the Navy. Beth had survived on intuition before, and she trusted her gut. She

1

checked the status of her M-57Z torpedo. The first of three torps in the tubes, it was running green and good-to-go.

It seemed as if each time the fleet returned to Refuge, there was a new model, and this would be her first time firing the "zulu" version of the fleet's most effective torpedo.

"Take your time, Fire Ant," Guppy—Ensign Jaret Minsk, their new flight leader passed on the flight net.

"Uh, roger that."

"Isn't he just the cutest thing?" Mercy asked on the S2S. "All bright and shiny new, and he wants to teach grandma to suck eggs."

Beth laughed out loud. Mercy's latest kick was resurrecting ancient sayings and proverbs, tr-ying to fit them in whenever she could, but at least this time, the shoe fit, if Beth could use an old one herself.

Guppy was so new his gold shoulder tabs were still covered in plastic. The CO had assigned him to be the new Fox flight leader, given the combined experience of Mercy and her, and this being his first mission was probably why they'd been assigned as angel for the operation.

But one thing three years' worth of experience taught her was that the FALs had their own plan, and now it looked like the butterbar's first mission would be hot.

Beth checked their positioning, wondering if she should let Guppy slide in and take the shot, but her AI gave him a 32.3% for his POS if she did that. It was all well and good to try and get him bloodied, but not at a detriment to splashing the enemy ship.

"He's just excited, Mercy. Cut him a little slack."

"Probably pissing himself in his flight suit about now."

Beth just shook her head. Mercy was . . . well Mercy. Beth loved her dearly, which was good as she'd married her little brother, but she lacked a little in military decorum . . . which was probably why Beth, despite initially being two years junior, had made First Class a month before her.

And that made her the second in command of the flight. Guppy, Mercy, Valkrye—NEP2 Letosa Mia—and her. With Guppy just getting his feet wet, the flight's chances of splashing the FAL were really on her shoulders.

"Splash one," Lieutenant Commander Knelton, the squadron XO and Delta Flight leader passed.

Beth pulled up the entire AOA. Some five-hundred thousand kiloklicks to their relative rear, Charlie and Delta had converged on the other three FALs and destroyed them. Kilo had already turned to follow Fox, but with the only other enemies gone, Mike started to wheel around as well, while the other seven flights started plotting courses back to the gate.

"You locked on, Dalisay?" the CO asked her.

Beth was either Fire Ant, Beth, or her flight number, Fox-2, to the rest of the pilots, but the CO always referred to her by her last name. Beth had wondered about that at first, but by now, it was just part of the landscape.

"Roger that. Unless things change, I've got an estimated time of launch in seven minutes, twenty seconds."

"Make the first one count. I want you heading back to the gate as soon as possible."

"Aye-aye. Will do. Fox-2 out."

"The CO wants us to be ready to get out of here as soon as we splash our friend up there ahead of us," she passed to the others.

"What? She told you that?" Guppy said, sounding hurt.

Crap. She bypassed him. Not a good way to build his confidence.

She wasn't going to lie, however.

"Yes, sir. She did." She didn't give him time to react, asking, "I'm wondering if you shouldn't slide up and get us into a Toro-yama. The FALs tend to get herky close to the end, and that might help cut it off if it goes that way. What do you think?"

The "Toro-yama" meant one position at the nose of the bull, two at the tips of the horn, and one at the tail. The "toro" in the formation was obvious, but no one could tell Beth why the "yama" had been tacked on.

It also focused power projection to the front while still having both a focus of main effort and security to the rear. In this case, it would pull the ensign up alongside Valkrye and leave Mercy behind.

"Really? You think that's what we should do?"

I'm laying it in your lap, Ensign. Make a decision.

"Your call, sir."

There was a long pause, and Beth was going to cut in, but Guppy passed, "Moving into Toro-yama now."

"Thanks a lot," Mercy passed on the S2S as the other three Wasps started to shift position.

"You weren't going to get the shot anyway," Beth told her. "And this gets him involved. You know what the Master Chief told us about training up the junior O's."

Beth had a love-hate—mostly hate—relationship with Master Chief Orinoco, but in this case, she was right. Guppy needed seasoning, and she and Mercy were the chefs.

"You're right. I don't want another Razor," Mercy said without her usual sarcasm.

Lieutenant (JG) "Razor" Singh had been their last flight leader . . . for all of two missions. He'd been splashed during their last mission, a victim of his bull-headed arrogance.

Beth checked the POS again. It was up to 51.2%.

Just a little more.

But she couldn't wait too long. The FAL was running, building up speed, and so their closing speed was slowing. Crystals didn't use external gates as humans did. Each ship was capable of jumping, although there still didn't seem to be any rhyme or reason as to how. This was the Holy Grail for the xenotypes, the various scientists who were trying to unlock the enemy's secrets.

The FAL was already up to .54C, at the lower end of the range before they jumped, but there were none of the vibrations that humans now knew meant a jump was imminent (and which lent weight to the theory that resonance played a part in their jumping).

She pushed the *Tala* harder, right to the edge of her compensator's ability to keep her from becoming a nasty red splash on the deck of her cockpit, something to be hosed out back on Sierra Station before the fighter was assigned to next the pilot up in the queue.

"I'm getting some harmonics," Valkrye passed after a few moments. "Code, uh . . . E-ninety-two-oh-six."

Beth didn't know that warning code offhand, but the flight leader did.

"You're out of balance, Valkrye. Break off and return to the gate immediately. Do not exceed 40G during your turn."

"I'm fine, Guppy. I can hang."

"That's a negative. The SOP says you're done. Break off now!"

"Wow. The kitten's got a little big-dog bark in him," Mercy passed over the S2S as Valkrye started looping around.

"Sir, do we continue?" Beth asked, ready to give the launch order. "I can take a shot now."

There was another pause, then, "Yes, we continue. Fire when your POS hits sixty-five percent."

Beth had planned on firing at 70%, but she wasn't going to argue. The CO wanted them back ASAP, so a few minutes earlier was in line with her intent.

She turned her attention back on the FAL, knowing that the others had her covered, watching for the slightest hint of vibrations. So, far, nothing . . . which was why she was surprised when the FAL blinked out of existence.

"What the hell?" Mercy asked.

"Fire Ant, what happened? Weren't you monitoring the QV-Band?" Guppy asked.

"Yes, I was monitoring," she snapped back. "Now get out of my ear and let me figure this out!"

Not how a first class petty officer responded to a commissioned officer, especially her immediate boss, but she'd worry about massaging his feelings later. At the moment, every hair on her body was standing at attention. Something was up, and she was sure it was something bad.

Beth had years of experience scanning planets, and while she'd had specialized scanners as a commercial scout pilot, the *Tala* was no slouch in that department.

"TSM-4, Kilting band," she ordered Rose, the name she'd given her AI.

Back at New Cebu, when the Crystals had been attacking the planet, Beth had identified the FALs by detecting the "bow wake" they left as they passed through the microparticles in space. Maybe she could do that again.

"No readings exceeding normal parameters," her AI informed her.

Beth frowned. She was sure the FAL had activated a cloak—maybe a more effective cloak, but the FALs were constantly innovating, and anything was possible.

"Ladder scan," she ordered Rose. "Identify anything out of point-zero-zero-four."

The *Tala's* AI started increasing power to each of the scanners momentarily to improve the chances of one getting a hit.

"Should I come back?" Valkrye asked, but barely registering to Beth as she concentrated on the mission at hand.

"That's a negative. Return to the gate. We've got Kilo inbound."

The comms telltale on Beth's display blinked a flashing lilac. The CO was slaving to her AI, but at least she was staying silent, letting Beth do her job.

Beth started her torpedo's nose-scan. It wasn't as sophisticated as the *Tala's* array, but it worked on a different arm of physics. It was theoretically possible for it to pick up something that the *Tala* missed.

But there was nothing. One moment, she was hot on the ass of the FAL, and the next, it was gone.

The only explanation was that it had jumped, but without the telltale vibrations that gave Navy pilots a few minutes of warning. She was just about to report back to the CO that she thought the FAL had jumped when her AI got a hit. The S-42, which was the military version of her old motusimeter scanner, had picked up something . . . but what?

The S-42 was designed to detect subtle degrees of motion, which was then fed into the *Tala's* targeting AI. Beth pulled up the readout. Just over the 0.004 delta parameter she'd set, it was detecting something. But the Kilting had been negative.

Beth stared beyond the HUD out into the black, as if her eyes could pick up what the *Tala* could not. Her intuition was screaming at her to get the hell out of there.

If the FAL hadn't jumped and was still out there, then they had something new, an ability to somehow slip past the microparticles without disturbing them. And that meant, there could be more of—"

"Break off, break off. RTB," she shouted over the net as she fired her first torp, based on the FAL's last course. She put full power into her P-18 meson cannon and fired, then started coming around to reverse course, pulling max G's as the *Tala's* compensators struggled to keep her in one piece.

"What's going on?" Guppy asked, confused.

"I think the crystals have a new cloaking system. Something we can't detect."

There was a pause, then the ensign said, "Uh . . . Fire Ant. I know you've got the experience, but if you can't detect it, then how do you know it's there?"

"Dalisay, are you sure?" the CO cut in on the S2S. "Could your target just have jumped?"

"No, I'm not sure. But something's going on. Check my S-42's readings."

"Damn, sista! What are you doing?" Mercy asked.

"I feel it, Mercy. Just get the hell out of here."

The flight was breaking up. Valkrye had already completed her turn and was heading back. Beth had just started hers, but Guppy and Mercy were still closing with the FAL . . . and Beth was sure it was still there.

"Dalisay, I just checked with Jean-Luc. He said that there's probably a flux in the Tam Coil. Nothing to worry about."

"Then where the hell's that FAL, skipper? It sure the hell didn't jump."

There was a long pause, and Beth could almost hear the accusation forming in the CO's mind. The great Fire Ant had finally broken. Too many dogfights, too many wingmen lost.

Maybe I have broken, but that's for the psychs to determine. Doesn't make me wrong, though.

Another alert blared in her cockpit. The P-18's beam had reached the position where the FAL had been when it disappeared. The area lit up like a Christmas tree, clearly showing a path through the void where the FAL continued after winking off her scanners, now turning as if to come back at the three Wasps. Something in her meson beam illuminated the FALs path, like luminescence in an ocean. Beth's torpedo got a lock and adjusted course.

"Kilo and Fox, RTB immediately," the CO ordered. "All hands, max power to your S-42s. Tolerance, zero-point-zero-zero-two."

Mercy and Guppy immediately started to turn back, the hunters becoming the hunted. And Beth could feel the Gs in a staccato pattern, like she was being used for a punching bag. Her compensators were pulsing as they strained. Any more, and she'd have to G-shot, something she really didn't want to do. She'd already done it four times, which had required a waiver to stay in the cockpit.

Her torpedo had lost lock, and it passed the location where the FAL had been. Beth hadn't expected anything else, but it was still a letdown.

"You holding up?" Mercy asked.

"The fun-meter's maxed," Beth said, glancing at her sister-in-law's stats. "Hey, you'd better put the pedal to the metal."

"I'm fine. I'll cut inside of you and beat you to the gate."

Beth wasn't so sure of that. Neither was her AI, but she decided not to say anything. If anyone hated the idea of G-shot more than Beth, it was Mercy. She'd done it three times, and the last time had been the worst. It had taken her a full three weeks to recover, all the time swearing it she'd never G-shot again.

Beth kept her S-42 trained behind her, tracking the FAL. She had to keep adjusting the scanner—it was giving her something, but it hadn't been designed nor calibrated to pick up the new Crystal cloaking. Still, she was pretty sure that the FAL was heading toward them. She considered using another of her torps, with all the unknowns, she wasn't able to calculate an accurate POS.

"We're picking up something," Lieutenant "Ogre" Mancivits passed to Guppy, keying Beth in. "I can't tell if it's what Fire Ant was seeing."

Kilo Flight had split into a blossom, each of the four fighters, breaking away from each other to loop back, timing it so they could come back together and give support to Fox Flight.

Beth shifted her S-42 forward, looking for any FAL sign. Nothing, and if it were there, then it would take a while for her scanners to see it.

"Upload it," she told the Kilo Flight leader.

Four seconds later, his data beam hit the *Tala*, and Beth's heart gave a lurch. Some hundreds of thousands of kiloklicks away, well beyond the FAL they'd been tracking, there was a mass of the same readings Beth had picked up. Her AI was trying to sort them, but without a baseline, it was working through probabilities, not established protocols.

All Beth knew was that there were at least a dozen, maybe more of the Crystal ships, closing in on the two flights. And that was just from what she could see. There was a lot of space around her, and there could be dozens more out there, intent on the kill.

"Light them up with your P-18s," she passed. "That seems to disrupt whatever cloaking they have."

"Roger that," Ogre said.

"Fox and Kilo Flights, you need to get back," the CO interjected. "Until we know the nature of what we face, I can't risk the rest of the squadron, and I can't let them get through the gate."

"Real nice, Skipper," Mercy muttered, but only on Beth's S2S.

But the CO was right. The one overriding rule the Navy had was that no FAL was to enter a gate. No one knew what kind of data they could glean from that, but humanity couldn't risk the chance.

If she had to, the CO would order the gate destroyed, even with Fox and Kilo on this side of it.

Kilo flight started firing their P-18 canons, and it was like the horror holovids, where the hero hears something and turns on the light, only to see a mass of zombies closing on on them. There were far more than a dozen, and they were coming from three directions.

This has been another trap, like too many the FALs had sprung before. Having lured Fox and Kilo Flights away from the protection of the rest, they were closing in for the kill.

Kilo Flight still had a clear shot to the gate, but it was going to be tight for the three Fox Flight Wasps. Beth ran four quick simulations, hoping the subsequent ones would give her a better result than the first, but the numbers didn't lie.

Guppy made it official.

"Kick G-Shot, and be ready to fight our way through. Uploading course now."

"Satan's balls," Mercy said over the flight net. "I don't think I can take it again."

"Shut the hell up, Mercy," Beth snapped. "You're going to do it, and now."

Beth didn't wait for a reply. She flipped open the red cover at the top of her display, then taking two deep breaths, flipped the lever. Immediately, molten fire poured into her veins and arteries, burning her up from the inside.

She'd been expecting it, but she still screamed in agony as the G-shot filled her body, giving it support, the screams choking off as oxygenated fluid filled her lungs to keep them from collapsing. Her arms grew heavy.

"Max G," she managed to subvocalize, and *Tala* leaped to obey like a racehorse out of the gate while the compensators screamed in protest. Without kicking G-shot, Beth would be a mushed red paste by now. While her body slowed down, four injections into her brain kept her functioning. It wasn't enough to be able to sustain 80Gs—she had to be able to fight.

Her brain felt as if it was cushioned in cotton, and her body felt leaden, but she could still function. As much as any Navy pilot, she'd done this before.

The three fighters pulled a tight turn to head back to the gate. "Tight" was relative, however. It was still going to take close to twenty minutes to come around, twenty long minutes as the FALs closed the distance.

And they would continue to close unless they were disrupted and had to deal with their own survival.

"Target anomalies with M-57. Fire when POS exceeds 30%."

"Instructions noted," her AI intoned. "Targeting."

A probability of success of 30% wasn't much, but it should give the FALs pause, if nothing else. As the AI's gained data points, the AOA started to coalesce around them. Twenty-two Crystals were closing in on the eight Wasps, most on the three lead Wasps from Fox Flight, but there were others trying to cut off Valkrye and Kilo Flight.

The *Tala's* alarm sounded as a FAL beamer swept past her. It took an effort for her to blink up her shield readings, and she grimaced when she saw they'd been degraded to 92 percent—from one strike.

It was time to show the FALs that this time, the prey had a bite, too. She considered the FALs that they'd been chasing first, but at one-against-three, it wasn't their biggest threat. The rest of the FAL pack was.

Beth started selecting targets, then hitting them with her P-18. Almost twice as powerful as the P-13 they'd replaced six months ago, they had the power to burn through the Crystals' shields . . . if they could be kept on target. The two forces were still far apart, and while the beams lost only a small percentage to spread, the time it took the beams to arrive gave the enemy time to juke.

No one knew just how the FALs detected the cannon fire before the beam arrived. Humans had quantum scanners that could register a shot, but there was no indication that the FALs had them as well. But the how wasn't as important as the why. They knew when the P-18s were fired and took evasive actions.

Beth could use that to her advantage, however. She targeted the nearest three FALs with a pattern she'd worked out a month before in a burst of mental productivity, but instead of lighting them up yet, she downloaded a program into her first torpedo and fired. The observed route would seem like a long-shot effort, one destined to fail

She hoped.

The *Tala* took another hit while her AI juked her out of danger. Beth checked her readings. Her shields were at eighty-two percent.

It was hard to focus while kicking G-shot, but it wouldn't matter whether her targeting worked or not if the FALs splashed her first.

Beth started slowly herding her three FALs with precisely aimed beams. She just hoped that they didn't realize what she was doing.

Mercy fired her first torpedo as the distance closed.

"You hanging in there?" Beth asked her as she continued to try and herd her targets.

"Yeah, right. Just dandy."

Mercy sounded like shit, but Beth didn't know how much was from kicking G-shot and how much was from Mercy being Mercy. There wasn't much that Beth could do about it now. In another fifty minutes, they'd be shooting the gate . . . if all went well.

Beth knew the FALs were doing whatever they could to keep that from happening.

She took another glancing blow, degrading her shields by another four percent.

"Concentrate, Floribeth," she muttered through clenched teeth.

Her head was aching like the worst migraine ever, something that hadn't happened during the first three times she kicked G-shot, surfacing on her fourth time—and now it was back in spades. Beth only hesitated a moment before giving herself another "brain boost" injection. She could almost feel it flow into her. Not that it diminished the migraine . . . it just made her more aware of it.

Her torpedo kept to its course, seemingly off-target.

It's time.

Her P-18 had been slowly herding her three targets, and now it was time to go full bore.

"Sending targeting now," she passed to Mercy and the ensign. "Give me what you can with your 57s."

"What for?" a blurry-sounding Guppy asked.

"No time to explain. Just do it."

Beth could see when Mercy fired and waited another moment before initiating the targeting pattern she'd entered for the P-18. Two of the FALs reacted just as she'd hoped, right when her torpedo adjusted to its pre-programmed course. She waited for a reaction, but the two FALs were still moving to avoid the meson beams that kept pushing them closer to the torpedo.

"What are you doing?" Mercy asked.

"Just watch and learn," Beth answered, struggling with the G-shot.

It was hard enough dogfighting the FALs with a clear brain, much less in a G-shot fog. Except they weren't really dogfighting. The three Wasps were running for their lives. Beth was just trying to give them a little more breathing room.

And then one of the FALs evidently saw the trap, swerving to enter Mercy's cannon fire. It would be taking damage, but that was better than what was about to befall the other.

Another forty seconds, and the second FAL started maneuvering, but it was too late. The hardened M57 torpedo had locked on, and it was running true.

"Splash one," Beth said as the FAL fighter was hit.

Normally, that gave her a thrill, but under G-shot, she didn't feel much. She idly wondered if this was a pilot's first kill under G-shot when it wasn't blind luck. If she hadn't made the calculations beforehand when she could actually think, there was no way in hell she could have come up with it now and gotten the kill in her present condition.

"Nice shooting," Guppy said. "I was wondering what you were doing."

The ensign was fighting to keep awake. Beth didn't have bio readings on him, but she knew he was fading.

"Are you set for autopilot?" she asked him.

"I'm . . . I'm OK," he said, slurring.

"No! Listen to me, Guppy. You're going to pass out. You've got to be on autopilot."

There was no reply.

Shit!

"Mercy, I need your spread. We've got to cover Guppy."

"Roger that."

A moment later, Beth had full control of their six remaining torpedoes.

"Maximize disruption, and fire," she ordered her AI.

Within twenty seconds, all six torpedoes were on their way. Maybe because they'd just lost one of their flight, the FALs seemed to overreact, maneuvering away while taking the torps under beamer fire. But the 57Zs were hardened, and they kept advancing.

Meanwhile, Beth and Mercy were coming around and heading for the gate.

Guppy wasn't.

"Guppy! Are you with me?"

Shit, shit, shit!

His Wasp was flying, but there was no response from him.

"We've got incoming, sista," Mercy said.

Beth tore away her focus with a huge effort. The FALs were biting back. Twenty of their round torpedoes were tracking them.

Her incoming alarm went off, and when she didn't respond, the *Tala* took over, initiating the close-in-defense system. P-18 farther out, then the rail-gun would kick in as any FAL torps closed within ten kiloklicks.

Was it going to be good enough?

"Run intercept calculations," she ordered her AI.

The numbers popped up on her HUD, but in her muddled state, she couldn't tell if they were going to make it.

Something gnawed at her mind, but it was too much effort to figure out what it was.

"Guppy, you with us?" she passed on the flight net as the ensign kept deviating from the course.

"I don't think he's conscious," Valkrye cut in, her voice, without G-shot, strong and vibrant. "Did you report it back to the CO?"

That's what I was supposed to do.

She opened up the squadron net, but the CO beat her to it. "We're on it. We're trying to slave his Wasp."

Which never worked once combat was engaged, thanks to the very shielding that kept them alive.

Beth had rescued Bull by taking him into her cockpit, and she'd grappled and then towed Mercy back after she'd been hit. Neither of those were done during G-shot, but that shouldn't matter, she thought in her addled state.

"I'm going after him," she told the CO.

"That's a negative, Dalisay! Stay the course!"

"I don't leave a wingman behind," Beth said, anger burning through the morass of her mind.

"We're working on it, but if you deviate, you are not going to make it back, and I'm not going to lose two of you."

Which means you've already accepted losing Guppy.

"Listen to her, Beth," Mercy passed on the S2S.

"You're not going to be able to slave his Wasp," Beth said, trying to calculate the numbers.

She took another hit, and the alarms destroyed her concentration. She didn't even check her shields. If they lasted, they lasted, and there wasn't much she could do about it.

Guppy was taking heavy damage. Like wolves on a crippled deer, the FALs were focusing on him . . . which was taking some of the heat off Mercy and her.

Beth couldn't let him do that . . . even as part of her knew he was most likely gone already, his Wasp's AI keeping the fighter flying. He was either dead or unconscious. G-shot saved lives, but there were many who just couldn't take it. Most were screened out at flight school, diverted from fighters, but even the best screening could fail.

"I'm going to grapple him," she told the CO and started to tell her AI to come to an intercept.

"Damn it, no, Beth!" Mercy shouted an instant before the CO said, "Belay that. I'm giving you a direct order. Proceed to the gate.

"Look, his shields are down to twenty-three percent. Another ten percent, and we think we can slave him. Leave it to us. We can't try to rescue two of you. Understand?"

"Beth, she's right," Mercy said.

Beth hesitated, the command to intercept Guppy on the tip of her tongue, but as she tried to think straight, the migraine came back with a vengeance. She screamed, either in pain or frustration . . . or maybe both.

Beth couldn't do any more. She was done. All she could do now was to trust the *Tala's* AI and hope that she and Mercy made it through before the gate was destroyed. Nine more minutes, and this would be decided, one way or the other.

She closed her eyes, only for a moment . . . and the next thing that registered was Sierra Station's traffic control was taking over, locking on to tow her into the hangar.

Beth was barely aware of Josh rushing to the *Tala*. He had to pop her canopy and unhook her harness.

"How's Mercy?" she asked, craning her neck to see three crew hovering over the *Louhi*.

"I'll find out, but we need to take care of you first."

She scanned the hangar. Valkyrie's *Strawberry Dream* was in the bay, but not Guppy's *Emma Jean*. She needed to find out what had happened, but she was just so tired.

"OK," Beth said before slipping into the welcome embrace of unconsciousness.

NAVAL HOSPITAL REFUGE

Chapter 2

"We really need to stop meeting like this," Doctor Wallis said, looking over her readouts.

"I just want the downtime," Beth said. "And to get that good hospital chow."

The Navy captain/doctor smiled, then, as he read the numbers, pursed his lips in a frown, his eyebrows furrowing together.

"Something the matter? You don't like the Sunday roast?" Beth asked, trying to sound as if she wasn't concerned.

But she was. This was the fifth time she'd kicked G-shot, and Navy regs required full physical evaluations and clearance after three times. She felt like shit, tired and achy, but that was no different than after her first four times.

"Joking aside, we really *do* need to keep meeting like this," he said. "Your F13-levels are higher than I expected, and I'm seeing more signs of mitochondrial damage."

"But, I'm still OK to fly, right? I mean, after I'm done here, of course."

The doctor raised his head to look into her eyes. "I'm not sure, Petty Officer. We won't know until after you get scrubbed a few more times. Maybe we can hoover out some of the rogue cells and get you on your way."

He gave a forced-sounding laugh, and for the first time, Beth was concerned about her future. If he grounded her . . .

It wasn't even worth considering. She was a pilot, pure and simple. Nothing else would do. Beth realized that each time she G-shotted, she increased the chances of cancer or a host of degenerative diseases, but that was all in the future, right? She could still fly now.

"And if you can't, sir? What's the worst-case scenario?"

"Worst case? Let's just forget that for now. I'm sorry to get you concerned about it."

Beth reached out and grabbed the doctor's forearm, making the IVs jerk in the holder. "I want to know."

Wallis gave her a contemplative look, then he shrugged his shoulders. "You can find this out easily enough, but knowing you pilots, you never do, all thinking you are immortal."

Or that we don't think we'll live to an old age, so what does it matter?

"And not just you pilots. The science is clear, but the brass disregards it. 'Operational risk,' is the excuse. Wartime needs.

"We don't have to upcheck you after three G-shots just as a precaution. Each time you do it, your body is damaged. You can recover from some of it, but the rest is cumulative."

Beth knew that, but as an abstract. Facing a possible grounding, it suddenly came into focus.

"I know about all the bad outcomes as I get older, but why do you ground pilots? We're all still young."

The doctor's eyes softened, and he said, "Because if you lose too much nervous function, you can't fly at peak performance. Not just physical, but mental."

"Was that what happened to Commander Jeston?"

"I can't tell you that, Petty Officer. Privacy regs."

Lieutenant Commander Jeston had kicked G-shot twice, and within a month, he was suddenly transferred to a desk job down on Refuge. Four kills, one away from ace, and he left after only three months with the squadron?

The commander had only G-shotted twice, one short of the required upchecking, and this was Beth's fifth time. Suddenly, she was feeling unsure of herself, and for the first time, apprehensive.

"But, like I said, let's just wait until we get some tests done. No reason to get yourself tied up in a knot right now. You've got another ten days with us, and we'll see what we can do," he said with forced cheerfulness. "I'm going to up your dosage of Benvid-22, and I think that might help. We're going to monitor you closely and see about getting you back in the cockpit. Can't have the one and only Fire Ant grounded, can we?"

"Thank you, sir. I appreciate that."

"I'll check back at the end of my shift, but like I said, don't worry. Just take it easy."

"Aye-aye, sir. I'll just take it a day at a time, and we'll see what happens."

But I'm still going to find out what I can, she told herself as the doctor left the room.

****

The promise of taking it easy lasted all of an hour. There wasn't much on the public undernet about the long-term consequences of G-shotting more than what they'd been taught at flight school. None of the details she wanted.

And that lack of knowledge was like ants crawling around her brain. If she didn't do something, she was going to go batshit crazy.

Beth was supposed to stay in the room, lying in bed while the drugs were working to heal her. But what could they really do if she broke her convalescence?

Every bed in this ward was self-powered, all the better for transferring patients when needed. Beth tipped over the IV stack onto the bed, then with her free arm, raised the back until she was sitting. She pulled the transport toggle free and started the bed forward. It took a few fits and starts—and slamming into the doorjamb—before she got the hang of it. She rolled out into the corridor. Two nurses were talking on the other side of the nurses' station, but neither gave her a glance as she rolled to the next room and pushed through the door.

The lights were low, and a holo screen was showing a nature show, the sound turned off. The room smelled astringent.

"Hey, sista! How's it hanging?" she asked as she rolled up next to Mercy.

Her sister-in-law opened one eye a crack, then closed it again.

"You look like shit," she told Beth.

"Thank you. I'll take that as a compliment."

Mercy remained silent, her eyes closed.

"What, no snappy comeback?"

"Not in the mood."

Beth frowned. Mercy *always* had a comeback. It was embedded into her DNA.

Beth reached out and took Mercy's hand in hers. There was no reaction.

"Hey, come on. This place isn't that bad. We get real chow tomorrow."

Mercy sighed and opened her eyes, but stared at the ceiling. "Don't you get tired of this?"

"What? The hospital? Yeah, I guess."

"Not the hospital," Mercy said, turning to look Beth in the eyes. "G-shot."

"Well, yeah. Of course. But it beats the alternative," Beth said with a little laugh.

"Satan's balls, Beth. I mean what it's doing to us. Every time, it kills a little more of us."

Which was exactly what had driven Beth out of her room and in to see Mercy. She wanted her sister-in-law's support, but it looked like Mercy needed it more than she did.

"We're still alive, Mercy. We're still functioning." She flexed one bicep, pointing to it with her other index finger. "See, still swole."

Mercy finally laughed at that. Beth was anything but a gym rat. As the smallest sailor on Sierra Station and where a third of the personnel were SEALs, she didn't like the condescending looks of the others while they threw around iron. No, she was in the twice-a-year fitness test mode. If the minimum scores weren't good enough, then they wouldn't be the minimum.

"What are you watching, anyway?" Beth asked, pointing at the display.

"Nothing."

On the screen, a single bee was doing some sort of dance, going back and forth along a line while the other bees crowded around, as if it was communicating with them. Beth vaguely remembered something about bees being able to tell other bees where the best flowers were. That was probably what it was.

It struck her as silly at the moment. All that effort, just to convey a simple message.

"Looks like us," Beth said, fluttering her hands. "Buzz, buzz."

But Mercy didn't laugh.

"Come on, don't you get it? I mean we fly Wasps, not Bees, but no one listens to us, right? They don't understand us, right?"

Mercy chewed her lower lip, a true sign that she was heavy in thought, and not about bees. Beth knew by now to leave her best friend be for a moment, not to push her. She sat in her rolling bed beside her sister-in-law, watching the holo, and waiting until Mercy was ready. And it paid off.

"Rock and I are going to have a baby," Mercy said matter-of-factly after a few moments

Beth's mouth dropped open. She leaned forward and stammered out nothing before she managed to get out, "You're pregnant?"

"No, of course not," Mercy said as if it was obvious. "Can't be pregnant on flight status. But . . . but I'm going to harvest my eggs . . . that is, if they're still good. This G-shotting . . ."

Beth leaned back, relieved. She'd thought Mercy had already done something stupid.

Except, would it be stupid?

Beth had no partner on the horizon, no hint of a future family. Besides, flying was her life. But she sometimes wondered about children. When she'd absorbed the radiation while saving the *Victory*, her own eggs might have been compromised. She might never be able to have children. At the moment, it didn't seem to matter . . . at least, she wouldn't allow herself to dwell on it. She had no control over that, so she refused to think of it.

"G-shotting doesn't do that," Beth said.

"How do we know? Last time, one of the nurses told me that the docs just don't know. Not many pilots have had to kick G-shot multiple times . . ."

And now, with war with the FALs, it's happening more and more often.

". . . but they think there could be cumulative damage."

Which is just what Doctor Wallis said.

Beth frowned and put her hand on her belly as if to protect it.

"So, what are you going to do?" she asked. "You going to get pregnant?"

"Can't. You know they aren't releasing any of us for the duration. Not enough pilots as there is."

Too many getting killed.

"But I'm going to ask them to harvest my eggs. Send them to Rock to, you know . . ."

"You're gonna have a creche baby?" Beth asked, shocked.

Illegal in several jurisdictions and frowned upon in most of the rest, Beth would never have believed her brother would go along with the artificial womb arrays.

"No! Of course not! No, Rock's found someone as a surrogate. Cece Paloma."

"My cousin Cece?" Beth asked.

"Yeah. She's agreed."

That didn't sound like the immature, fashion-conscious cousin Beth remembered, but who knew?

She reached out and took Mercy's hand again. "What brought this on, Mercy? Your eggs are fine, you know."

"What if I don't make it back next time, Beth?" Mercy asked, squeezing her hand tightly? "Every time we go out, we're one step closer to the reaper. If I . . . I have to leave something behind when that happens. Rock needs something, too. Someone."

"Now you're just being melodramatic, Mercy. You're the Red Devil, too tough to die," she said with a forced laugh.

"No one's too tough to die. We've seen it happen too many times."

She let go of Beth's hand and turned to the wall.

Beth just stared at her back. She was right. No one was too tough. And she understood what Mercy wanted.

The question was if luck ran out and the FALs splashed her, would there be anything left in the universe to say that Beth had been there?

SIERRA STATION

Chapter 3

"Why's the *Tala* deadlined?" Beth demanded of Petty Officer Second Class Josh Frye, her plane captain, as she barged into the petty officer's lounge.

She'd only arrived back at Sierra Station fifteen minutes ago, and as expected, had immediately gone to check on her fighter. To her surprise, the *Tala* was still deadlined.

Josh flipped up his goggles from the immersive he was playing and hit pause.

"Nice to see you, too."

"I'm serious, Josh. You've had three weeks. Why can't I fly?"

"Seven-six-ninety-two isn't going to fly again. At least not with the squadron. She'll be refurbished and sent to one of the defensive squadrons."

Seven-six-ninety-two? Why is he referring to the Tala by her tail number? And a defensive squadron? What was up with that?

"What the hell are you talking about?"

"New fighter arriving tomorrow. The November version. We're getting ten in."

"But the Novembers are not scheduled for another two years."

Josh shrugged, then said, "I guess they pushed the schedule up. Might just be that there's a war going on, you know."

Holy crap. A November?

Despite herself, Beth started getting excited. From all rumors, the November wasn't just an upgrade. It was essentially a new bird.

She had a passing twinge of sadness about the *Tala II—* no, the *seven-six-ninety-two*, she had to remind herself. It was bad luck to keep a name on a fighter you no longer flew. But the old fighter and she had gone through a lot together, and she— *it*—had always brought her back alive.

Still, a November?

"What have you heard about it?" she asked, barely containing herself.

"All the same rumors you have," Josh said.

"What's wrong with you, Josh. A gearhead like you, and aren't you excited?"

A slow smile spread across his face. "Oh, hell, yeah! I can't think of anything else. Why do you think I'm playing Zombie Hunter now? If I don't keep myself occupied, I think I'll go crazy before tomorrow."

Beth wasn't a huge game player, but she knew Zombie Hunter. All sailors knew Zombie Hunter. And with her excitement building, maybe she needed a diversion as well. She wondered if she could play all the way until the new Wasps arrived. She certainly wasn't going to get any sleep tonight.

"You got another feed?"

"I'm playing dead. You up for that?" he asked, pulling out another pair of AR goggles.

Of course, Josh would be playing as a zombie. He was one strange dude when you got down to it.

"That's good enough for me," she said, taking the goggles. "Let's eat some human brains."

Chapter 4

Beth took a deep breath, a smile on her face. The new *Tala III* was . . . friggin' amazing! Her old birds were the cream of space fighters, thoroughbreds among plow horses, but this . . . the November Wasps were a huge step forward.

"How'd she do?" Josh eagerly asked as she popped the canopy.

"Purred like a kitten. Got her up to 53 Gs and never felt a thing. Turns on a dime, too."

The compensators on the old Wasps were good to 40 Gs—anything higher required G-shotting. This was an over 25% improvement, something that Mercy . . . and yes, Beth, too . . . would appreciate.

And the *Tala* needed it. With new Tumkyin thrusters, the fighter had a much tighter turning radius, which increased the G-forces on the pilot.

Josh leaned into the cockpit and reached across Beth, almost pushing her back into the seat as he held his scanner to the Performance Diary. There was a soft beep, and millions of bits of data were transferred, enough for Josh to analyze every aspect of the test flight.

"Uh . . . how about getting off of me, you big oaf! You're crushing me!"

"Oh, sorry," Josh said as he scuttled back. There was a thud as he landed on the hangar deck.

Beth unhooked, then stood. The Novembers had a larger cyclotron under the fuselage, and that raised it almost twenty centimeters. Given Beth's short stature, that might make it more difficult for her to get in and out of the cockpit, but it had turned out to be a godsend. That extra twenty centimeters made it more difficult for the other pilots to simply hop in and out, too, so when the cockpit opened, a recessed ladder formed in the skin. No more steps rolled into place for her to get in and out of the fighter.

Josh stood next to the *Tala*, beaming like a kid on Christmas morning. As soon as her feet hit the deck, he motioned to the yellowshirt to move *his* Wasp to her slot so he could go over every centimeter of her. The hangar at Sierra Station wasn't the same mad choreographed ballet of a battleship hangar, but the Navy was hidebound in its traditions, and only yellowshirts were authorized to move spacecraft after they were powered down.

"Oh, Lieutenant Farris wants to see you," Josh said over his shoulder as he watched the yellowshirt, a new petty officer Beth didn't recognize, hook up the *Tala*.

Of course, the squadron maintenance officer would want a report. The *Tala* was only the second of the ten Novembers to take its shakedown flight. But he could wait a minute or two. She watched as the *Tala* lifted off the deck.

The November Wasps looked much like their earlier versions. A little taller, a little bulkier. A bigger undercarriage, all to house a bigger cyclotron and to carry an extra torpedo.

More powerful-looking, but still a Wasp. And this was hers. The same "*Tala*" and star on the prow. Her name. Josh's name. And thirteen diamonds, symbols of her thirteen kills. She felt a surge of pride flow through her.

Just short of four years ago, she was a commercial scout pilot, flying her Hummingbird, and in insurmountable debt to Hamadani Brothers. Now, she was the leading Navy pilot in a life-and-death struggle with an alien enemy.

"Nice-looking bird there, Fire Ant," a voice said from behind her.

Juggler—Lieutenant Commander Huk Denepa, and the Bravo flight leader—was looking past her with appreciative eyes. "How'd she handle?"

Not only was she the Navy's top ace, but she had the respect of her fellow pilots. This officer, who probably wouldn't have given her a second glance back in her explorer scout days, was treating her as an equal.

"Like a dream. When do you get yours?"

"Not for a while. I'm hearing eleven more weeks."

"Still plenty of time to snap in before we deploy."

"Yeah, but I want it now!" he said with a laugh. "I can't wait."

"It'll be worth it," she said as they both watched for a few more moments.

"Well, I've got to report in to Lieutenant Farris."

It was a strange world where she could call Lieutenant Commander Denepa "Juggler," but the maintenance officer was "Lieutenant Farris." But Juggler was a pilot, and Farris was not. Pilots used each others' callsigns, but the rest of the squadron was still "regular" Navy.

"Take it easy," Juggler said.

Beth made her way into the station proper and down the corridors hewn into the asteroid. She'd long ago gotten used to the exposed rough rock. This had become her home.

The maintenance spaces were in with the other shops, at the far right of the station, and closer to the solar panels that provided most of their power. It took her ten minutes before she entered the maintenance office, nodded to Lisa McDill, the leading petty officer for the division, and then knocked on the lieutenant's hatch before sticking her head in.

"Sir?"

"Oh, Dalisay. I need to talk to you about your shakedown flight, but the CO wants to see you ASAP. Go down and see her, then come back, OK?"

It took some effort, but Beth managed to keep from rolling her eyes. Why hadn't the CO just sent word to her as she was landing? It would have saved her the long walk to the maintenance spaces.

"Roger that," she said, then gave Lisa a wry smile as she walked out and back into the corridor. She wasn't sure why the CO needed to see her, and for a moment, she had a sinking feeling that something had gone wrong with Mercy. Her sister-in-law hadn't recovered from her funk and was being held at the hospital for a few extra days. Finding out that the CO had managed to slave Guppy's Wasp, but then lose him to a FAL torpedo seventy-three seconds before shooting the gate to safety had been the final nail in the coffin, and she had sunk into a huge depression.

Mercy seemed strong to others, but there was something very vulnerable in her best friend, and Beth hoped against hope that the docs could help bring Mercy back. Now, she feared for the worst.

She picked up the pace, barely responding to greetings as she hurried to the squadron office spaces. It was a breathless Beth who entered the CO's outer office.

"Petty Officer Dalisay, I'll let the CO know you're here," a new non-rate said, pointing at the bare bench up against the bulkhead. The office spaces were not the exposed rock of most of the station. Flat-white panels covered the bulkheads and overheads, while sound-deadening tiles made up the deck. Beth had to sit on the edge of the bench for her feet to reach the tiles as she wondered what the CO wanted.

It's not Mercy, she kept telling herself.

But she couldn't keep that fear at bay.

It was along ten minutes or so before the CO's hatch opened. "Come on inside, Dalisay."

Commander Tisha Nbento was Beth's third CO and the one who puzzled Beth the most. She was tactically sound, but on a personal level, Beth couldn't read the woman. That wasn't a positive or a negative. But because of that, Beth was always slightly ill at ease around her.

"Take a seat," the CO said before she returned to her desk. She picked up a folder, then handed it to her.

Beth gave it glance before looking back at the CO, not sure if she was supposed to read it or not yet. The CO gave her a slight nod, so she opened it and picked up the single plastisheet. It was a printout of a naval message, and she scanned past the heading information to the subject line:

Subj: Promotion of NEP1 Floribeth S. O. Dalisay, 445287923, to Warrant Officer

Her first reaction was relief that it wasn't Mercy, but then it sunk in and . . . *what?*

Beth looked up at the CO, who finally began to crack a smile.

"But I never applied," she stammered out. "And I just made first class."

"Three years as a pilot, Dalisay, performing your duties in a satisfactory manner. I think we can all agree that you've done that.

"And you don't have to apply. Needs of the Navy."

Beth looked back down and stared at the order, sure there was a mistake. But no, it looked legit as far as she could tell. On the first of the month, in twenty-three days, she would be a warrant officer.

"I've got permission from Fleet to frock you as of today," the CO said.

"What, ma'am? Frock me?"

"We can pin you today. You won't get paid until next month, but you'll wear the bars, and you can change your uniform."

Beth was in shock, her mind a muddle. A happy muddle as it started to sink in, but a muddle nonetheless.

"I don't have any officer's uniforms," she said.

"You will by tonight. As soon as the orders came in, I had Tracey Ruiz at the White Duck make some up for you. Just the initial outlay, and they'll be on the seventeen-hundred shuttle. You'll have to pay for them now, of course. Officers don't get free uniforms," she said with a laugh.

"If it is all right with you, I'm opening the club tonight, and we can do the ceremony there."

"All right with me?"

"Sure. You're paying, after all. It's your wetting down."

Beth shook her head. Of course, a promotion wetting down was paid for by the person getting promoted. Tradition was that she had to spend at least as much as her raise would be.

How much is that? What do warrant officer get paid?

But that didn't matter. That this was a surprise was the understatement of the year. Of course, Beth had hoped to make warrant officer some time, but that had been for the future. Not now. To think that she could be frocked tonight was mind-blowing.

But Mercy won't be here.

If she was going to be promoted, then her wingman, her best friend, her sister-in-law, had to be there. She wouldn't forgive Beth if she went ahead with it tonight.

"Uh . . . ma'am, I appreciate this, but can we do this later? Another day?"

"I'm afraid not. It's tonight or never."

"I was thinking that after Petty Officer . . . what, ma'am?"

"Oh, not the promotion. That's on the first of next month. But the frocking. The wetting down. If you want to do it with the Stingers, I mean."

Beth stared at her CO. She understood the words, but not what they meant.

"Ma'am?" she squeaked out.

"The other set of orders. They came with your promotion orders."

Beth looked back at the folder. There was another naval message there. She put down the promotion message and picked up the next one.

To: Promotion of NEP1 Floribeth S. O. Dalisay, 445287923
From: Director of Personnel, Second Fleet, Navy of Humankind

Subj: Transfer Orders to VR-75, FS Valley Forge, Task Force 3/32

What? I'm getting transferred?

Beth hurriedly read on. It was true. She was getting transferred to VR-75 for further attachment to Task Force 3/32 for a period of no less than 180 days. The rest of the message was administrative measures, to include the date . . . which was tomorrow.

Beth felt the blood flow out of her face, and a hole formed in the pit of her stomach. The Stingers were her home. She'd never been in another squadron after flight school. And it didn't make sense. The Stingers were due to forward deploy in four months.

Why are they taking me? Is it because I'm getting promoted? I'll turn this thing down if that's the reason.

Then something she'd read caught her attention again: VR-75. That wasn't a Wasp Squadron.

She looked up at the CO and asked, "VR-75. Isn't that—"

"A reconnaissance squadron. Yes. It looks like you're going to be a scout pilot."

"But . . . but why? I fly Wasps."

The CO shrugged. "I don't know. I'm not privy to anything more than what you just read. It could be that the detachment needs some Wasp firepower, but I'm guessing you're going to fly Mosquitos."

"I don't know how to fly them," she said, grasping at straws.

"You didn't fly one at flight school?"

"Well, yes."

The Navy only had two single-seat craft, Wasps and Mosquitos, both built from the same basic platform, not that it would be obvious to the casual observer. The controls were the same for both. But the similarities ended there. The Mosquito was barely a spacecraft, with a constrained cockpit, an underpowered, but stealthy powerplant, and a stripped-down fuselage. The biggest difference, however, was that the "Skeeter" had no weapons. Zip. Nada. Where the Wasp carried its weapons, the Skeeter carried sensors.

There was no question that Beth could fly a Mosquito. She just didn't want to.

"I still don't understand. Why not just assign another scout?"

The CO's eyes softened for a moment, and she quietly said, "You've seen the casualty rates, right?"

And Beth's heart fell. Of course, she was aware of the toll in scout pilots. They were supposedly the cream of the crop, taken from the ranks of the best fighter pilots, and their operations tempo had increased. Rumor had it that they were searching for the FALs' home planet.

Here she was, feeling sorry for herself that she was being yanked out of her comfort zone when the scouts were seeking the enemy in unarmed craft.

"And it makes sense, Dalisay. You were essentially a scout once, right, in the civilian sector? You flew, what was it? Kyocera Hummingbirds?"

"Yes, ma'am."

"And you've proven yourself as a fighter. I'd say you were made for the mission."

The CO's right. Time to wear your big girl panties, Floribeth.

She looked at the orders again. The adminspeak was confusing. "How do I get to the *Valley Forge?*"

"You're flying yourself."

"On the *Tala?*"

"Yes . . . uh, wait. Not the new one. I need that here. Your old frame is still here. I've already got Chief Wilson working on it."

Beth felt like a scab had just been torn off her heart. Not only was she leaving the squadron, but they were taking away her brand-new *Tala?* They were really piling it on.

But it made sense. If she just needed a taxi, then her old *Tala* would do, and the new *Tala* . . . she would have to be rechristened . . . could be given to another fighter pilot— someone who would actually be fighting.

"You'll be leaving at ten hundred," the CO said. "You'll be getting your gate routing by Fleet right before that.

Beth nodded. It was out of her hands, she knew.

"So, is the wetting down on?" the CO asked.

Sorry Mercy, but I can't wait.

"Yes, ma'am. Let's do it."

****

"You know, I ain't about to be saluting you," Mercy said before draining her glass, then putting it upside down on the table.

"I'll write your ass up, Petty Officer," Beth said as she looked around the club.

It was packed, both with the squadron officers as well as the SEALs. And all were drinking—on Beth's tab. Not just the officers. As the senior officer aboard the station, the CO had opened it up to all the enlisted pilots as well.

Beth had blanched as she tallied up the costs—she was still being paid as a first class, and the bump in pay to warrant officer wasn't that much—but she was glad all the pilots were there.

Especially Mercy. She'd been scheduled to be released from the hospital in three days, but she'd done what she does, and she'd showed up with a smile and carrying Beth's new uniforms.

She glanced down at the khakis she was wearing. Most of the others were in their flight suits for the pilots, their station utilities for the SEALs and staff. She felt . . . odd, she guessed it was. Like a poser. One hand rose to her right collar to touch the bar there.

"Yeah, your WO bar is still there, sista. It didn't fall off."

"Fire Ant, Fire Ant!" Bull yelled out from across the club, raising a half-full stein of beer.

The entire place broke out chanting her name.

Mercy kicked her leg, and reluctantly, Beth stood as the others cheered. She looked at them all, her wingmen, her tribe. This was where she belonged, not off as a scout.

"Stand up!" Lieutenant Jac Islador yelled.

"Very funny, Flapjack. At least I didn't have to just get a bigger flight suit," she yelled back, rubbing her stomach.

Laughter filled the room, and a hand snuck out to pour what was left of a cider on Flapjack's head.

"Satans' balls! Shut the hell up and let her speak," Mercy yelled.

Beth took a deep breath, gathering her thoughts.

"I want to thank you for coming to my promotion."

"Promotion? There was a promotion? I just came for the free booze!" one of the SEALs shouted.

"Well, you better get it quick. According to my tally, I'm about spent-out."

There were good-natured boos and jeers, but Beth was already going to have to cut the payment she sent to her mother next month.

"Next round's on me!" Bull yelled above the din. "You all know Fire Ant saved my worthless life, right!"

"We know," at least six people shouted in unison.

Beth felt her face redden in embarrassment. Beth had detested then Chief Warrant Officer 2—now CWO3—Nicolescu when she joined the squadron, but ever since she'd brought him back from his dead Wasp, they'd gotten closer. Whenever Bull got drunk—and it looked like he was way past there—he'd remind everyone about the rescue.

"As I said, thank you for coming to my promotion," she started again, wanting to cut Bull off. "I really do appreciate it.

"I'm going to miss you all—"

She stopped in horror as there were surprised shouts from the other pilots.

Beth whipped her hand over her mouth, then looked over to where the CO was standing. Beth had just broken opsec. To her surprise, the CO just nodded.

"I just found out myself. I've just got orders to . . ."

The CO had just given her permission to explain herself, but that didn't mean she could give out the details.

"I'm going TAD for a while. Not sure how long."

"Another photo boondoggle back on Earth?" Cossack asked.

"If I told you, I'd have to kill you. Or at least get Lieutenant Singh over there to kill you for me."

"Anything for you!" the muscular SEAL said.

"But I'll be back before the deployment. Can't let Motown pass me in kills, you know."

There was more laughter, and everyone looked expectantly at her for more until she said, "That's it. Finish your drinks, then let Bull pay for the next round."

There was another round of cheers, and Beth sat back down.

"You wormed your way out of that one," Mercy said. "Almost spilled the beans."

"Doesn't matter much, anyway. I don't know what I'll be doing."

"Bullshit. Scouts take the best, and you, sista, are the best."

Beth gave Mercy a sideways glance, wondering if her sister-in-law was punking her, but for once, she seemed serious.

"You're going to miss me, you know," Mercy said.

"I know I am," Beth said, trying to hold back the tears that threatened to flow.

"Then come here and give me a hug, *Warrant Officer*."

Beth slid her chair over and gave Mercy a tight hug. "You stay safe, sista, and if you want that baby, I'll do my best to spoil my niece rotten."

"That'll be your job, Beth. But you'll have to come back safe and sound to do that. So, I may just be a peon petty officer, but I'm your sister, and I'm ordering you to come back, you hear?"

"Aye-aye, ma'am," Beth said, the tears falling on Mercy's shoulder.

FS VALLEY FORGE

Chapter 5

The *Valley Forge's* tractors brought the *Ninety-two* onto a gentle landing on the flight deck. No *"Tala."* Beth had already transferred the name to her—to what had briefly been her—Wasp, and somehow, it just didn't seem right to bring the name back.

Beth had even wiped the personality on the *Ninety-two's* AI.

Immediately, a yellowshirt moved her mule into position, her impatience evident as she waited for Beth to get out. With a sigh, she popped the canopy. Taking one last look around the cockpit, she stood up, turned, and began the awkward slide to the deck. There wasn't a Josh to move up her stool, and there weren't the built-in steps the Novembers had.

She knew she looked ridiculous, and she felt eyes on her butt as she slid belly first, her foot questing for the deck. Beth let go and dropped the final twenty centimeters. At least she kept her feet.

"I've got my seabag in the CYCL," she told the yellowshirt, holding the woman up. "I need it opened."

Which a yellowshirt couldn't do. Opening any of the compartments took a redshirt armorer. This spaceman wasn't going to be delayed, however. "We'll forward it to your quarters, ma'am. So, if you can please step aside . . ."

Beth hesitated. The *Valley Forge* was a *Rorke's Drift*-class battle cruiser with over 2,000 sailors and Marines on board. If it was anything like the *Victory* had been, then there was a good chance that her bag might never quite make it to her.

But the yellowshirt had already powered up the grapple, and the *Ninety-two* rose a few centimeters off the deck. Beth resisted giving the Wasp a pat, then turned away, wondering if that was the last time she'd see the fighter. It had served her well and kept her alive, but its time was past.

A slightly overweight chief walked up to her holding a scanner. "Ma'am, if you will?"

This "ma'am" was going to take some getting used to. But she stopped while the chief scanned her eyes. She didn't know why that was necessary. How many warrant officer pilots were expected to arrive by Wasp, and a specific Wasp at that which had been scanned and logged by the ship's traffic control system?

The chief took a quick look at the readings, then said, "Welcome to the *Valley Forge*, Warrant Officer Dalisay. I'm Chief Julio, the detachment admin chief. If you'll follow me, I'll take you to our spaces."

"Good to meet you, Chief. But my bag, it's on my fighter. We put it in the CYCL."

"Don't worry about that. I'll make sure it gets to your compartment.

I hope so. Otherwise, it's going to be a long haul washing my panties in the sink every night.

The two made their way through the bustling hangar deck, where redshirts, yellowshirts, and greenshirts performed their daily ballet of launching and recovering fighters, transports, drones, and all the other craft that called the *Valley Forge* home.

"Hey, Fire Ant!" someone called out as they wended their way to the hatches into the ship proper.

Expecting to see someone she knew, instead, it was a yellowshirt petty officer she was sure she'd never met.

"Welcome to the *Forge!*" the petty officer said, giving her the raised index and little finger salute popular in the Beckter Alliance. Two others around him stopped what they were doing as well to wave.

Beth was still surprised by her notoriety. It was easy to forget that she'd had her fifteen minutes of fame . . . twice. Aboard *Sierra Station*, and even back on the *Victory*, she'd just been part of the squadron. But here on a new ship, it was different. The CO had told her that her orders were not being promulgated except for those with a need-to-know, but either than meant what looked like the entire ship, as more sailors stopped to look at her, were in the need to know group, or she'd just been recognized.

Beth waved back self-consciously, and she was relieved as they exited the hangar and made their way back through the corridors, past a fierce-looking Marine guard, and into the secured spaces. They went down two decks, then around one of the lateral decks, before the chief scanned his eye, and a hatch opened.

"You're already supposed to be in the system," he told her. "Should have checked it and let you open it, though."

I can still do that. Just close the hatch and let me try it, she thought, but left it at that.

The space was small and bare, which she expected—just not this small. Two pilots in the subdued tan scout flight suits, one sitting on the edge of the single desk and the other standing beside him were staring at her, as was a second-class petty officer. That was it. Three people—four, if she counted the chief—were it.

The lieutenant commander (Beth saw as he sat up straighter) said, "Welcome to the detachment. Glad to have you here. I'm Rip. This here," he said, pointing with a hooked thumb to the second lieutenant commander, "is Twister."

Twister looked at Beth with dead eyes, no expression on her face at all.

"You've met the chief, who runs the day-to-day of the detachment, and this is Petty Officer Salz, our systems tech. There's one more of us, Yancovitch, our plane tech, but she's in the bay now doing her job."

"Five people?" Beth asked, surprised. "And one plane tech? You've got three Mosquitos, right?"

Twister gave a half-laugh, half-snarl, and Rip said, "That's all it takes. We get the support we need, but the fewer people around us, the better. Chief takes care of whatever has to be done to support us. Yanc keeps the Skeeters operational. Salz handles the systems. And the two of us, we do the flying. Three now, with you."

Beth was used to the almost three hundred sailors it took to keep the Stingers flying. This was only a detachment, true, but still, six sailors, including her? This wasn't the Navy way.

Beth had flown with scouts before, on the *Victory*. But she'd never looked into how many sailors were in that detachment. She would never have believed it would have been so few.

"You have flown a Skeeter, right? I know what it says on your records, but it wouldn't be the first time that the flight school pencil-fucked someone's checklist."

"Yes, sir," she said before wondering how to address him. Normally, as a fellow pilot, he'd be Rip, and if he was a squadron commander, he'd be "sir." She had no idea how the Navy, and specifically the pilots, treated a detachment commander.

"I can't say I've very proficient in the frame, though."

Rip waved that off with a dismissive shake of his head. "You've flown Wasps. Same controls for the most part. You just need to learn the package."

By package, Beth knew he meant the suite of scanners that were the raison d'etre of the scouts.

"And you'll be starting right now. Salz here is going to escort you to your Skeeter. I want you to spend the next few hours with him getting to know what you're carrying.

"Tomorrow, you and I are going on a check-ride, then you'll have your first mission."

If the small number in the detachment was not the Navy way, then having a mission within a day, with a new frame, was not even close to it. It was the antithesis of the Navy way, and it was all a little much for her. Two days ago, she was doing a shakedown with her new Wasp, and expecting to train for another four months before she could see action. Now, by tomorrow, she'd be on a mission.

"Am I allowed to ask you what my mission will be?"

"They didn't tell you?" he asked, looking up at Twister in confusion.

"No, sir. I was just told to join up with you. I didn't even know for sure that I'd be flying a Mosquito until you just now mentioned it."

"Shit, what else would you be flying in a *scout* detachment?" Twister asked, scorn dripping from her voice.

"I've flown Wasps in support of scouts before. Saved one or two, you know," Beth snapped. She was tired and mentally numb, and she didn't know how she'd pissed off this pilot.

"We know your record, Fire Ant," Rip said, putting a hand on Twister's forearm.

"And the mission?" Beth asked again.

"It's the mission of the entire fleet of the Navy's scouts. We're going to find the FALs' home planet.

SECTOR JK-59011

Chapter 6

Beth checked her lanterns. She was lined up and ready to jump the gate. She'd always been a little nervous each time through, but this was worse. Yes, a Mosquito was built upon the same frame as a Wasp, but no, it was not nearly as maneuverable. It really didn't make much of a difference. Cruise liners used gates, after all, and her old Hummingbird explorer wasn't even close to the capabilities of her new ride. But it wasn't a Wasp.

"Oscar Leader, jumping in forty-five seconds," she passed to the Wasp flight leader.

"Roger that, Sierra-Three. Good hunting."

Just be there if I need you.

Rip had been good as his word. Nineteen hours after arriving on the *Valley Forge*, Beth was on a mission.

At least there hadn't been a learning curve as to flying the Mosquito. Her control interface was the same as on a Wasp, minus the weapons panel. No need for weapons aboard a scout, right? It wasn't a combat craft, seeking to engage the enemy. And the FALs honored the chivalric code and would never attack an unarmed craft, right?

But, of course, they did.

Beth had been shocked when Rip gave her the butcher's bill of scout pilots. No fewer than one-hundred and twenty-four of them had been lost, 54% of the Navy's total. Beth wasn't the only Wasp pilot being pressed into service; she was just the first to be pulled from the Stingers, which had previously been untouchable.

Without weapons, a Mosquito was vulnerable, but the Navy wasn't sending them out on suicide missions. Each Mosquito had the very best cloaking technology, even when it affected maneuverability. The powerplant, for example, was a toned-down version of the FC engines in Wasps. Besides being toned-down, the thrust was directed out of adjustable nozzles, each a marvel of masking the electrons that were being ejected. What there weren't were the Tumkyin bow-thrusters that gave the Wasp such great maneuverability.

So, as Beth approached the gate, she didn't have quite the same capability to correct her course, and as anal as she could sometimes be, that worried her. She knew she was worrying too much. Her old Hummingbird never missed a gate . . . but then again, she had taken it through large commercial gates, not a tiny thing like the one ahead of her.

Come on, Floribeth. Calm down.

She took a deep breath. The lantern, an old term whose origins were lost in history, indicated she was still on course. As long as she was in the digital, but ever-decreasing cone, she'd pop out on the other side, where her mission would begin.

The Mosquito had no weapons, and without the weapons, didn't need the massive heat dissipation systems as well. No fire turds. The Navy took away some of that space to make the craft smaller, but the rest was taken up with the array of equipment that put her scanners on her Hummingbird to shame.

Her mind had been numb as she listened to Salz, with pride that threatened to burst through his chest, explain each and every system aboard the scout. There was no way Beth could comprehend all of that in a mere few hours, but luckily, she didn't have to. The array was controlled by an AI. Beth's job basically boiled down to turning the system on after jumping the gate, then turning it off before coming back through.

This really could be entirely automated.

And without the FALs, drones could take up much of the slack. With the FALs, the drones were being lost at much higher rates than the manned Mosquitos.

Beth mentally counted down the final five seconds before she shot the gate. As always, she felt—or if she listened to the scientist-types, imagined she felt—the pass through the gate. It made sense to her, however, that she felt something. For a nano-instant, even as quick as it was, her nose was in one sector of the galaxy while her ass was back at another.

And then it was time to get to work. She turned on the system, letting it do its thing before she pulled up the area scanner, the same one that was on a Wasp. The system was quiet—nothing showed up on her HUD.

Which probably meant that this was not the FALs' home planet. But it still had to be checked out. For all she or anyone knew, even the so-called experts, the crystalline FALs might live underground, only emerging to traverse space . . . and attack humans. That was one train of thought, at least.

After over sixty missions as a civilian scout, however, Beth had a finely-tuned instinct on what was in a system, and this, she knew, was a dry well, to use her old civilian terminology. That wasn't to say there weren't FALs here. They had a habit of showing up where they weren't expected. But this wasn't their homeworld.

Which would be just too coincidental if Beth, already a noted pilot, found the FAL homeworld on her first mission. According to Rip, the scouts had already searched over two thousand systems, all selected by huge AIs on Earth and San Marten as having the best probability of being their target. But while two thousand seemed like a lot, it was nothing when considering the galaxy had over ten-billion stars, and that was assuming the FALs were from humanity's neck of the woods.

They had to assume that, however. Anything else made finding their homeworld impossible instead of just improbable.

"Oscar Leader, I'm in-system. Confirm upload."

"Roger. Uploading uninterrupted. We'll be here if you need us."

The data Beth was gathering could be worthless, or it could be immensely important, too important to rely on her getting back alive. So, huge amounts of data, terrabytes a second, were uploaded over the Navy twinned comms back to Fleet Headquarters. But twin comms could be temperamental, especially if her Mosquito suffered damage, so as a backup, the data was being sent over a simple laser back through the gate to the Wasps.

"So, let's just see what's here," she said as she inputted her course. In a Hamdani Brothers Hummingbird, surveying the system would take five or six days, depending on how far out she entered the system.

With her Mosquito, she'd be doing one looping sweep, returning though the gate in just over six hours. She'd be back before the *Valley Forge* served midrats. Then it would be time to try and catch some sleep until tomorrow's mission. This was to be her routine for the next however long.

The pace was a killer—literally. Beth had wondered what happened to her predecessor, thinking he'd been killed in combat. She'd been shocked to find out he'd dropped dead of a heart attack. Thirty-one years old, physically fit, but the constant "on" had been too much for his body to take.

As much as Beth hated the gym, she'd made an immediate mental note that she had to hit it. She didn't have any false hopes that she'd live out the war, but she didn't want to go like that.

Nor did she want to go out without a fight, as statistics would indicate might be in her future now. Being a Mosquito pilot had a worse survival rate than flying Wasps.

Beth tried to keep her mind off the morbid thoughts as her scout approached the target planet, but there wasn't much to keep her occupied. She ate a bite of TN bar, more to just be doing something than for hunger, and took a swallow of MD-3, "Muddy-Three," the tepid, orange-flavored energy drink with which the Navy fueled their pilots, missing Josh something fierce. Totally against regulations, he'd always found a way to get Coke into her Number Six nipple.

Her battle display remained quiet. There was nothing in the system that it could detect. Her scanners were going full-bore, however. The upload stream was active. She didn't have the knowledge to make much sense of it even if she could see a readout, but she imagined it was a whole lot of nothing.

Beth's course wasn't directly at the target planet, but rather to the gas giant farther out from the system's star. She'd let the planet accelerate her Mosquito, slinging her around to her target, Planet Number 4. She'd use that planet's gravity to adjust her course to head back to the gate. The concept was sound, and one she'd used as a commercial scout. Then, it was to shorten her trip back out to her gate. Now, it was to gain speed to outrun any possible threat.

The approach to the planet went off without pause. A huge storm, bigger than ten New Cebus, roiled on the planet's surface as she shot past, beautiful and dangerous. She thought she could see flashes of lightning. If that was true, then they must be unimaginably huge. Beth set her display pickup to the giant, mesmerized, just watching the slowly shifting show.

And then it was on to her target. Planet Number 4 was not very impressive, especially when compared to its huge neighbor. Tans and browns were prevalent, and there was no sign of an ice cap. A dead planet, from all appearances. In the past Beth could hope there were minerals there that would earn her a bonus. Now, unless there were FALs there, this trip was a dry well.

She whipped around the planet, letting it nudge her back toward the gate. She was now at .65C, which was pretty good after shooting a gate.

"Maybe you're not so bad after all," she said, patting her control console.

Yes, the gate placement and where the planets were in their orbits were advantageous, but still, she was booking it.

Her lantern cone was pretty broad at the moment, but she still checked that she was within it, trusting her AI to take her closer.

She was contemplating whether she should eat again when her alarms went off, causing her heart to jump into her throat.

Three bogies appeared on her display, rising from one of Planet 3's moons. Beth didn't need to wait for her AI's analysis. They were FALs, and despite all her stealth capabilities, they knew she was there.

"Oscar Leader, I've been painted by three FALs," she sent back through the gate on the laser comms.

"Do you need a guardian, Sierra-Three?" the flight leader asked.

"Wait one."

Beth had already been plotting courses. The Crystal ships were a third-way across the system orbital plane. There was no doubt in Beth's military mind that they knew she was there and were out to intercept her. But the question was whether or not they could. If Beth had come in on the other side of the system, it would have been an easy intercept for them. But as it was . . .

Beth ran through several courses of action. It would be close, but if she could goose a little more out of her ride, then whip around Planet 4, she should be able to get a line on the gate ahead of the FALs.

Should.

"Oscar-Leader, I'm going to bug out. I think I can keep ahead of the FALs."

"Send me your situationals."

The flight leader was not in Beth's chain of command, and for a moment, she bristled, but common sense sunk in. The data she was already sending had to do with the system and didn't include anything to do with flying her Mosquito. As her security, he had a vested interest in knowing the threat.

"Roger that. On its way."

She linked her situationals to the transmitter, then turned back to refining her course of action. If she had her new Wasp, the numbers would be in her favor. Hell, if she had her old *Tala*, they looked good. But a Mosquito's detuned FC engine didn't have the oomph to push the craft past 37 or 38G on its own. No G-shot, which was either a relief or a worry . . . and Beth wasn't sure which.

Given her present speed and course, that should be enough to get her heading to the gate well in front of the three FALs, but not by a comfortable margin. She settled in to wait, watching the approaching Crystal ships, running new projections every couple of minutes.

The holovids showed space combat taking place in minutes, but this was the norm. It would take more than an hour before things started to shake out. This was the most difficult part of being a fighter pilot, Beth thought. She tried to force her mind to remain calm, but it wouldn't cooperate. She started chewing on her already almost non-existent fingernails.

Hell, don't just sit here. Do something.

She ran a few more progressions and saw an opportunity to give herself a slight advantage. She had to override her AI, but unlike when she first discovered the FALs, this time, she didn't have to shut it down. She just had to confirm her intentions before tweaking her course just a bit to take her closer to Planet 4.

That was one good thing about the Navy: they understood that pilots sometimes had to take some chances.

"That's cutting it a little close, Sierra-Three," Oscar-Leader passed. "You're going to be outside the safe envelope."

Envelopes were calculated with built-in safety cushions. When she'd first run into the FALs, she'd taken her scout past the envelope to get more speed, and that was in a Hummingbird, not a Navy Mosquito.

"I know what I'm doing," she passed back, and to her surprise, the flight leader didn't come back to argue. Maybe her status earned her some latitude, even from a Lieutenant Commander.

I think I know what I'm doing, that is. This Skeeter can take it, right? she asked herself.

The numbers were good, however. The FALs continued to accelerate, but unless they had some heretofore unknown boost, she should be free and clear in another thirty-two minutes and heading for the gate. If they chose to fire on her, though, that would be different. Some of their torps might be able to catch up to her before she reached safety.

Finally, she was entering Planet 4's grasp. Still no sign of torpedoes as she started to sling around the planet. Her heading changed, but the FALs just kept proceeding on their course.

Beth's stress started fading. This would have been the optimal time for the FALs to fire their torpedoes. From here on out, Beth, with her already-generated speed would be stretching the distance between them. Maybe the FALs weren't even combat fighters. They could be commercial craft of some kind, if the FALs even had them.

Beth watched as the Mosquito came to her new course—back to the gate and safety.

"On my way home, Oscar-Leader."

"We'll keep the lights on, Sierra-Three."

Beth took a deep breath, then settled in. She realized her mouth was dry and took a big swallow of Muddy-Three. It wasn't Coke, but it sure tasted good at the moment.

Another two hours, and she'd be home free—until the next mission.

Behind her, the three FALs had finally altered course on an intercept, but they were falling farther behind her. There was no way in hell they could catch her now.

The relief was like a wave, and everything since leaving the hospital caught up to her. In the old days of planetary air travel, they called it jet-lag. Now, it was just exhaustion, mental and physical. Her eyes got heavy, and she started to nod off . . . to be brought crashing awake as her alarms sounded.

It took her a moment to orient herself. She'd only been out for five minutes, but that wasn't her concern. To her left, three more FAL craft were converging, and she didn't need to run the numbers to know that they'd be able to cut her off before she could reach the gate.

Why did they wait until now to show themselves?

And then five more FALs appeared on her HUD, but far to her right on the orbital plane, from around an asteroid belt.

She'd been closer to the asteroid belt on the way into the system, but if they hadn't reacted, then it had to be because her cloaking had hidden her until she got in closer. The FALs hadn't known from where she'd entered the system.

"Son-of-a-bitch!" she shouted.

The three behind her had never been intended to splash her. They'd been there to flush her out, to get her going one way or the other. And now that she'd committed, the three coming at her were the threats.

"Sierra-Three, I've got three FALs coming at you."

With a wry grimace, Beth opened her display to take in the entire system so that Oscar Leader could see.

"Shit. That's eleven."

"Yeah, shit," Beth repeated. "Are you going to be able to come save my ass?"

There was a moment of dead silence, then finally, "We can't let the gate be compromised."

What the hell? Then why did you even come? Beth thought, getting more than a little angry.

"Wait one," the Oscar flight leader passed.

"Yeah, right, asshole!" Beth said, then cut the voice connection. A moment later, the LED flashed, but she ignored it. She didn't want to hear his excuses. His four-fighter flight wasn't much against eleven FALs, and part of her knew that, but another part, a bigger part of her, was royally pissed and feeling more than a little abandoned.

If she was going to somehow get out of this, it was going to be on her and her alone. But how? She had no more tricks up her sleeve.

She pushed the Mosquito as hard as she could, but there wasn't much left in her FC powerplant. The detuning it needed to become stealthy took away its punch. Five G-shots or not, Beth would gladly take a sixth at the moment.

Her laser comm link kept flashing. Beth was tempted to connect just to give the Oscar Flight leader some well-deserved hell, but she didn't have time for that as she wracked her brain for a course of action that would at least give her a shot at survival.

Twelve minutes and fourteen seconds after picking up the second three FALs, one of them fired a torpedo. It was still a long distance away, but if she'd had any hope that these were some sort of commercial craft, that went right out the window.

She was surprised that more weren't fired, but it only took one for a kill.

The Mosquito didn't have weapons, but it was not entirely unprotected. Beth went over her options. She had her shields, which gave some protection against energy weapons, and the same neck-cracker helmet as she'd worn in the *Tala*. Against torpedoes? She had the six decoys, and not much else.

That rather made up her mind. But she was going to wait. No use playing her hand early. The fact that the FALs had only fired one torpedo meant that they only had one, or they were waiting to see what sort of defenses she had before engaging with more.

Beth figured it was the latter of the two.

And she wasn't going to jump the gun. Anything to delay the inevitable.

With a sigh, Beth hit the record, leaving a message to her mother, to Rocky, and then to Mercy, and sent it off. This was the fourth time she'd recorded such messages, and she knew them by heart by now, but this time, she knew they'd actually be released.

To her surprise, she wasn't sad so much as angry. Beth knew this day would come, but she'd really rather it happened after she'd at least met Rocky and Mercy's baby. But the FALs— and fucking Oscar Flight—had determined otherwise.

Her luck had finally run out.

She wasn't going to go quietly into the night, however. She was a Wasp pilot, the best of the best.

Beth tracked the incoming torpedo, waiting . . . waiting . . . knowing that her Mosquito—and her—would be blown into their component atoms if it hit her. At only two-thousand kiloklicks, Beth released her first decoy, then kissed her silver cross and held her breath. But the damned thing worked. The torpedo locked onto the decoy, detonating less than a minute later.

"Well, damn!" she said, laughing in relief.

She hadn't been sure the FAL torpedo would fall for the decoy. Evidently, whatever stealth capabilities her Mosquito had, it had been enough so that the decoy had captured the torpedo's lock.

Her relief was short-lived, however. Within two more minutes, three more torpedoes were on their way. The FALs had seen what had happened, and they would have made adjustments. Beth had five more decoys, but she could not count on them. She'd try, of course, but she was rational enough to know what her chances were, chances that got even smaller when three more torpedoes were launched to follow the other spread.

The gate was still over twenty minutes away. The first torpedoes would reach her in a little over eight minutes.

Beth's tactical scanners were still set for the entire system, so she ratcheted down the focus to the incoming torpedoes. She didn't know what she expected to find, but she was grasping at straws. She needed something, anything, to give her a chance.

But there was nothing. She was going to have to use the decoys again, which were not as effective against salvos. And then there was the fact that she only had five, and there were six torpedoes on her ass.

Her alarm went off again, her HUD bathed in a soft red glow. One of the FALs had fired its energy weapon at her, but her shielding was holding. Beth didn't bother to try and juke. A Mosquito was not very maneuverable, and anything she did just made the gate that much farther away. Every juke added time. And if she somehow got past these six torpedoes, then she needed every saved second she could generate.

Constant incoming would degrade her shielding, but she'd be long dead already before it completely collapsed.

Her mind raced, reaching for anything. She wildly considered ideas before discarding them as useless.

"Satan's balls!" she shouted aloud, using Mercy's go-to curse, when she realized there wasn't much she could do.

But she wasn't going to roll over and die. If her decoys worked, then she'd just have one more on her, and she could try to dive. The FALs, their torpedoes, and Beth were generally on the system's orbital plane. The gate was only slightly "below" it. There was a small chance that she could "dive" at the last moment, too tight for the oncoming torpedo to fire.

It was a crap plan, but the only plan she had. Beth took out her cross again, letting it ride on her chest. She knew she needed all the help she could get.

Another energy beam painted her, and the shield numbers started falling faster. Beth just laughed. She'd give up a year's salary to live long enough to have to worry about the FALs punching through her shielding.

And then the first three torpedoes were on her. She programmed one decoy to keep on her present course, then popped it and two others, and at the same time, slightly adjusted her course.

Beth kissed her cross, then put it in her mouth as the enemy torpedoes closed with her.

To her amazement, it worked. Maybe it was the cross, maybe it was good-old human technology, but the FAL torps dutifully followed, the closest one detonating a mere 78 klicks—that was klicks, not kiloklicks—away.

"Ava Maria," Beth muttered, happy, but surprised.

It's got to be the cloaking. They know I'm here, but they don't have a good lock on me.

Beth had tracked Crystal ships by detecting the disturbance they made flying through space. Maybe this was the FALs doing something similar. She should be dead meat by now, but somehow, she was still alive and kicking.

But for how much longer?

The next salvo of torpedoes was closing fast, and she had only the two decoys left.

"Calm down, Floribeth. Breathe!" she said around the cross that was still in her mouth.

She took five deep breaths, but it didn't do much. Her nerves were on fire with anticipation.

She waited. One minute until impact. Thirty seconds until impact.

She raised a hand to touch the cross, then fired off her last two decoys. Two of the torpedoes shifted their course, while one kept on. Maybe it didn't know exactly where she was.

At eighteen seconds out, the torpedo gave a slight course correction, and Beth knew she was made. Immediately, she turned toward the computer while she "dove."

Her alarms were screaming for attention, but Beth's focus was on that last torpedo, and it started to alter course. At five seconds, Beth knew she'd done it. The FAL torp could not turn quick enough, and Beth shot past at just over twenty-seven klicks.

If she'd waited another second, she'd have been dead.

But she was alive, and she whooped in her cockpit. Against all odds, she'd done it.

She adjusted her course back to the gate and picked up the torpedo . . .

"What the . . . ?"

When a human torpedo lost lock in a head-to-head confrontation, it usually just kept going at its last heading. The damned FAL torpedo was pulling an amazingly tight loop, something beyond what any human ship or weapon could do. The forces on it had to be amazing.

Beth ran a quick calculation, but she knew in her heart the answer. As long as the torpedo remained under power, it would catch up to her five minutes before she could reach the gate. And with them both going in the same direction, another dive wasn't going to work.

Her AI noted three more torpedoes being launched, and Beth just shook her head.

I guess this is it.

She took another long swallow of Muddy-Three, wishing it was Coke. She deserved to go out with a nice cold one.

Beth half-heartedly ran some progressions, but she really didn't know for sure what was going to splash her: the single torpedo that had made its turn and was now on her tail, the three that were just launched, or her shields failing.

It turned out to be the three new torps. Her shields were down to twelve percent as the three closed in. Beth kept her scanners on them, wanting to face her demise.

At eighty-three seconds out, one of the torpedoes started to drift, which surprised Beth. She watched it for a moment, then to her amazement, it wasn't there anymore.

"Their torps have a stealth mode now? Why bother?" she muttered.

Then the second one ceased to exist. And the beam weapons targeting her her cut off.

Beth flipped her HUD to full coverage, and like a beacon of hope, three Wasps were bearing down on her.

Beth flipped on the comms, and almost immediately, Oscar-Leader cut in, "Finally! You're alive! Your guardians are here, so you didiho back. Oscar-four is on the other side of the gate to escort you back!"

"You came," Beth said, suddenly ashamed of herself.

"What? Of course, we came. We're your guardians, Fire Ant. Now get the hell out of here!"

Beth hadn't been watching the torpedo on her ass once it became evident that the other three would reach her first. As the Wasps splashed the third one in the last salvo, and took the closest FALs under fire, it was suddenly back into play. She did a quick progression, and it was going to reach her two minutes before she could shoot the gate.

"I've still got one on my ass, Oscar-Leader."

"We've got it in hand," the flight leader said. "You just link up with Oscar-Four."

And he did. One of the three Wasps was painting the torpedo, eroding it's shielding while the other two charged the three closest FALs.

Two against three were not good odds, but Beth knew why one of the four Wasps had been left behind. The FALs could not be allowed to shoot the gate.

Beth felt even guiltier now for thinking they were going to abandon her. They had come to her rescue, and it very well could come at a heavy cost, one Beth didn't want on her shoulders.

For a moment, she was tempted to break off, to stay with the three, but then what? She had no weapons, no way to contribute. And she'd be throwing away their sacrifice for nothing.

"Happy hunting . . . uh . . . Oscar-Leader."

She realized that she'd never even asked for his callsign, or that of the others in the flight.

"Roger that, Fire Ant. And you owe us a beer when we get back."

"With pleasure. Now get some!"

Beth just hoped that she'd have the opportunity to pay that debt.

With tears forming in her eyes, she lined back into her lantern. Three-minutes and nineteen seconds later, Beth shot the gate and was back into safety.

FS VALLEY FORGE

Chapter 7

"That should do it," Yanc said, checking the upload.

"And that's going to fix the fact that the FALs spotted me?"

Yanc shrugged, then said, "Maybe. Maybe not. And even if it does, it'll only work until the FALs do their next upgrade."

Beth had a momentary image of a FAL pilot out there somewhere, watching as a Crystal tech upgraded its torpedoes.

That was assuming that FALs even had techs or did downloadable upgrades. No one knew yet how the FALs lived. The Xenologists were now sure that the FALs "grew" their ships, but much of their tech was still a mystery.

Which begged the question as to how Beth's Mosquito was already getting an upgrade. If humanity didn't understand Crystal tech, how could they develop something to counter it, and in this case, hours after her engagement.

It might as well be black magic, for all Beth knew. She wanted to ask Yanc, but the plane tech was already moving to upgrade Rip's Mosquito.

Yanc was no Josh. Her former plane captain took an almost unnatural love for his fighters, babying them at every step. Yanc was evidently competent enough—she would never be assigned to the scouts if she wasn't—but it seemed to Beth that she thought of her work more as just a job. There was no evident pride in her work.

Beth watched her for a moment, wanting to ask more about the upgrade, but she was due out in two more hours, and if she wanted chow first, she'd better get to the galley. With a shake of her head, she started to leave the scouts' small hangar.

"Bad luck, you know," Yanc said over her shoulder from where she started working on Rip's Mosquito.

Beth stopped and looked back. "What?"

"Bad luck. You haven't named her. No wonder you got painted."

Beth raised her eyebrows in surprise. She hadn't expected the ever-efficient, officious petty officer to believe in superstitions.

No, she hadn't named her Mosquito. She didn't want to. If she did, it would be as if she'd cemented her position as a scout, and this was only temporary. Her place was with the Stingers, not here, and she wanted as few ties as possible to the squadron.

She waited for something else from Yanc, but the plane tech was silent, watching as the latest and greatest tweak was downloaded into Rip's scout, the *Halberd*.

Odd name for a craft, she'd thought when she'd read the name on the Mosquito's prow.

Just under the name was "Lieutenant Commander Hector 'Rip' a'Dat," and under that were his six kills as a fighter pilot, followed by the number 35.

Two more missions, and he'd get the "40" on the *Halberd's* prow.

Scouts didn't rack up kills, so they got a new "nickel" after each five missions.

She looked back at her Mosquito. Her name was there, still looking odd to her with "Warrant Officer" instead of "Petty Officer First Class," and her thirteen kills, but no plane name.

Beth was going to have to think on that, but her stomach took that moment to growl, and Maslow's Hierarchy reared its head. She did not want to be eating TN bars during the next mission, so she left the hangar and headed to the galley.

A girl has to eat, right?

With a ship the size of the *Forge*, the starboard forward galley, the one to which the pilots were assigned, was almost always serving chow.

"Fire Ant!" a voice called out, a voice she recognized.

"Oscar Leader!" Beth said, striding over to where he was sitting with a huge plate of a pasta of some kind.

"It's Halo," he said, standing and holding out a hand.

"That's Ringworm, and the dumb-looking guy there is Tool," he said, pointing to a young petty officer who looked up at Beth in obvious hero-worship and a large, pale-looking CWO2.

Beth shook their hands, then asked, "And Oscar-Two?"

"Marmot's in sickbay, already bitching, but fine."

Marmot had taken off for the remaining FAL during Beth's rescue, and she'd had to G-shot to get back through the gate before it was blown. Now she had at least two weeks of recovery before she'd be able to fly again.

Beth had felt guilty about that when Rip had told her, but at least all four had survived. Beth had lost wingmen before, but the thought that any of them could have died to save her had been a burden weighing heavily on her until the three had joined her and . . . "Tool," Beth remembered . . . the Wasp pilot who had waited on the other side of the gate, ready to destroy it if need be, leaving the rest of the flight on the other side.

Now Tool was busily shoveling in some gravy-covered mystery meat as if someone was going to take it away from him.

"I just want to . . . you know . . ."

Halo waved her off. "It's our job. What you do, well, that takes big cajones."

Beth smiled slightly, as always, when she heard that common Navy phrase. No, she didn't have actual cajones, but she appreciated the greater meaning.

"How does it feel?" Ringworm asked.

Beth turned to the woman, a tall and lanky redhead who was now towering over her. "How does what feel?"

"Thirteen kills," the young woman said.

"Pardon Ringworm here," Halo said, pulling on the taller pilot's arm to get her to take her seat again. "She was rather star-struck when she heard not only were you here on the *Forge*, but that we were your guardian angels for the last mission. She's a little . . . enthusiastic, I guess you could say."

Ringworm reddened and looked down, refusing to meet Beth's eyes.

"Why don't you slide over and give Fire Ant a seat?" Halo asked Ringworm. "I mean, if you want to," he added to Beth.

She looked around. People tended to eat with their own units, but none of the other five in the scout detachment were there, and she hated to eat alone, so she nodded and said, "Thanks. Just let me get my chow."

She went back to the line, dialed up a Bocaburger, salad, and Coke, and then sat down with them. She still felt guilty that she had essentially accused them of abandoning her, and it was hard to meet their eyes, but the three of them didn't seem to notice. Talk gravitated to the new Wasps, and when Beth said she'd flown one, they started excitedly grilling her for the details.

Before she knew it, Beth was at home with them, feeling like she was part of the team. That wasn't something she'd felt with her own detachment.

Not everyone welcomed her . . . starting with Twister and including some of the other pilots. Not that many said anything, but their stares were hard to misinterpret.

And she understood that in part. They'd trained together before the deployment, melding into a team. More importantly, they'd fought together, and Beth was an unknown, despite her reputation.

Add the fact that at the moment, the fighters were in a support role to the three scouts, well, that was bound to have an effect. Beth was thankful that these three pilots from Oscar flight felt differently. And it was good to be talking shop. That crossed all group boundaries. Pilots everywhere loved to talk about their rides.

"Uh-oh, here comes Wyma," Tool said, interrupting Beth's rendition of the new Wasp's exhaust specs. He put down his fork and wiped the gravy from his face.

Beth turned to see a short woman, almost as short as she was, with close-cropped hair, ebony-dark skin, and a determined look on her face. More importantly, she was in a generic blue jumpsuit without an indication of rank or specialty.

"Who's she?" Beth asked, turning back to see the other two joining Tool in leaving.

"We don't abandon wingmen in harm's way, but that's Wyma, and we've already been grilled. Your turn in the breach," Halo said as he took one last swig from his coffee and moved to return his tray.

The woman didn't even glance at Halo as she locked onto Beth. Almost as short as her, the woman was a good 20 kilos heavier, and one hip bumped into the back of another seated pilot as she approached. The sailor started to object, turned and saw who it was, then quit and went back to his meal.

The woman walked past Beth, took Halo's abandoned seat, and without an introduction, asked, "Warrant Officer Dalisay, what ancillary observations do you have about your recent contact with the NSB-1s?"

Beth just stared at her for a moment in surprise. She looked around the galley. No one was paying attention to them—in fact, those closest seemed to be going out of their way to ignore the pair.

Everyone on board the ship was there fighting the FALs—the NSB-1s, the official term the woman used—but still, questions about missions were generally done in secure spaces, not in the open like this.

"Who . . . who are you?" Beth asked.

The woman frowned, then said, "Wyma St. Croix," as if surprised that Beth didn't know.

"Wyma St. Croix" didn't mean anything to her, and Beth was feeling uncomfortable. No one was jumping up to intercede, but still . . .

"What's your rank?" she finally asked.

"I'm not Navy, of course," the woman, Wyma, said. "I'm with the DAA."

Beth raised her eyebrows. The Department of Alien Affairs was a newly-formed organization within the Fourth Directorate, in charge of all things Crystal. Beth knew about the organization, but except for seeing one of them at a weapons brief, she hadn't yet had any contact with them.

"Interspecies communications," Wyma added.

That was even more surprising. There was a group trying to communicate with the FALs?

Good luck with that!

"So, if you can answer my question now, that would save us both some time," the woman said.

"What was the question again?"

It looked like the. . . scientist? . . . tried unsuccessfully to keep from rolling her eyes, but she asked, "What ancillary observations did you make during the course of your contact with the NSB-1s?"

Which made no sense to her. "Ancillary observations?" What the hell were those? She knew the meaning of the words, of course, but not in this context.

"Uh . . . should this be . . . I mean, here, in the galley?" she asked, more to buy her a bit of time than for anything else.

Wyma looked around, shrugged, and then said, "They all know me."

I guess she really isn't Navy.

Debriefs weren't done over Bocaburgers and in public.

If that was the way it was going to be, then who was Beth to argue? But she still didn't know what she was supposed to tell the woman.

"I'm not sure what you want. All of my sensors were recording, and all of those made it back. Nothing was lost."

"Yes, I've gone over them."

"Then I don't know what you want from me."

Wyma sighed, then reached over and picked up Beth's Coke, took a swallow and put it back. Beth didn't say a word and tried to control her shock. This woman evidently had no boundaries.

"I guess that was to be expected. You military personnel tend to rely on training to handle every possible situation. If this happens, you do this. If that happens, you do that. At least you believe that you do. In my experience, pilots, in particular, rely on intuition more than other personnel. Jules and Hahn were right two centuries ago, but I don't think they went far enough. My theory is that those of you who let your intuition guide your actions are more successful in combat, and as a result, survive longer. You, by virtue of being the most successful fighter pilot in the Navy, would—should—be a prime example of someone who uses axiomatic analysis—"

"Excuse me? Axio-what?"

"I'm sorry. I can get sidetracked, Warrant Officer Dalisay." She paused, took a breath, and then continued. "Axiology is the science of placing values on observations, which, in turn, leads the human mind to intuition. And as intuition is quicker than rational analysis, it allows those so gifted, if I can use a layman's term, to quickly develop a more accurate assessment, allowing them to react quicker and with better results. Ergo, in your case, survive more battles with the NSB-1s."

She leaned back with a pleased look on her face.

Beth thought back at her training for a moment, the hours and hours in the simulators practicing every type of conceivable fight, of the training exercises in her Wasp during deployment workups. The Navy way was to drill until fighting became second nature, so that for every situation, there was a by-the-book answer. The Navy way wasn't to rely on intuition. Intuition could be a good thing, but it could also lead a pilot astray. And by astray, that meant get them killed.

"But doesn't, uh, forgoing facts in favor of intuition run the risk of getting things wrong?"

The satisfied smile faded from Wyma's face. "It hasn't hurt you. Your test scores indicate a highly intuitive mind, and you seem to have survived quite well."

"I've been lucky," she said, but wondered as to how this woman had gained access to her personality screening scores. Just who was she?

Wyma waved her hand in the air as if brushing away a fly.

"There's no such thing as luck. It has no basis in science. Cause and effect, Warrant Officer. We've known that for millennia. You make your own so-called luck."

The woman was passionate on what she was saying. Beth could see it in her eyes. But that didn't make it true. Facts were facts, and intuition was . . . just that. And that still didn't explain what the woman wanted from her.

"I didn't have any axio . . . intuition on my mission. Just my instruments."

Wyma leaned her head back and laughed at that, revealing the most amazing set of teeth Beth had ever seen. No teeth were that perfectly aligned.

"Of course, you had intuitive thoughts. Everyone does. I just wanted to talk to you to find out yours as you've proven yourself to be better at using your right hemisphere."

It took a moment for Beth to digest that. Was there something more to just plain luck in why she was still alive? Sure, she knew she was technically a good pilot, but no better than some others who had been lost.

"And that will help you . . . how?"

Wyma let out the long sigh of someone who had given her reasons a thousand times, probably to uncertain recipients. "We have analyzed every emission from the NSB-1s, along every known wavelength. We've run them through our AIs, through some of the planet brains, trying to understand what the NSB-1s are saying, so-to-speak."

Planet brains? This is something big.

Planet brains were just that. They were the computer networks that ran planets, self-contained and shielded against any attack, and so they were rarely used for anything else.

"Brute analysis is getting us nowhere. I think we need to try an axiological approach if we're going to try and make a breakthrough."

"And you think this will work? That we'll be able to talk to the FALs . . . I mean the NSB-1s?"

Wyma laughed again, a deep, heartfelt chuckle, and said, "No."

"Then why do it?"

"Because it might work. And nothing else we're doing has proven itself effective."

Beth nodded. The woman had a point.

"I still don't know what I am supposed to tell you," she said, however.

"Tell you what. Why don't you just let me ask you some questions? Don't think about the answer, don't consider anything. Just says what comes to your mind. Is that acceptable?"

This was a lot for Beth to take in. Not so much about her mission. If she could offer anything that would help the war effort, of course, she was willing.

What struck her most was that there might be a reason she'd been successful so far as a pilot. She'd faced death too often and come out on the other end alive. And that weighed on her. Why not Commander Tuominen, or Swordfish? What had she done to deserve it?

Beth was proud of being an ace, and she was proud of being the top Navy ace, just a local Cebuano girl made good. But there was always the guilt hanging over her, the knowledge that she was simply lucky.

She'd always been intuitive throughout her life, as a child, as a civilian explorer pilot, and as a Navy pilot. Shutting off her AI back in her Hummingbird, when she first ran into the FALs, had been intuition after all. If she'd stuck with the SOP, she'd have been killed right then and there.

Halo and the rest of Oscar Flight either feared or were exasperated by the woman sitting across from her. Beth intended to wring the woman dry and learn what she could, if Wyma would give her the time.

"Ask away. I'll be happy to help."

An hour later, wrung dry with Wyma's piercing line of questioning, Chief Julio tracked her down to get her back for her next mission.

Beth took a final sip of her now-flat Coke, looked at the barely touched Bocaburger on her plate, and thanked Wyma.

She had a lot to think about.

Chapter 8

Beth took off her helmet and sat in the cockpit for a long moment, rubbing her forehead, trying to somehow forestall the headache she felt forming. She'd just returned from her nineteenth mission in sixteen days, and she was exhausted.

Another dry run. After almost buying it on her first contact as a scout, it had been a whole lot of nothing. She really didn't want to do another death run, but this was getting old quickly. High tempo, physically and mentally demanding, and nothing to show for it. The detachment's morale was in the dumps, with each of them barely speaking as they passed each other coming back or going out on their next mission.

And it wasn't just the detachment. The entire ship was getting antsy. It was a battle cruiser, with an entire Wasp Squadron, Marines, and over two-thousand crew, and they were doing nothing. The entire ship's raison d'être was to support the three scouts, and the inactivity was getting on everyone's nerves.

Fifteen battle cruisers and quite a few more smaller capital ships had the same mission, plying space as single vessels, leaving potential combat to the task forces. But one of the battle cruisers, the *FS Somme*, had just been engaged in a major battle when it was jumped by a FAL force. The *Somme* had taken serious damage, but it had survived, and there was grumbling within the *Valley Forge's* crew that their mission was useless, and without supporting vessels, they were at a much higher risk. They didn't want to be skulking about the far reaches of space but rather be taking it to the FALs as part of a full Navy task force.

The yellowshirt waiting to move her scout stood looking at her with an exasperated look on his face. Beth gave him a nod, and with a sigh, started to extract herself from the confined cockpit. No nice receding steps as with the Novembers, but the scout was also lower to the ground. Still, Beth had to hop down to the deck, and after the inactivity of the last nine hours, she almost stumbled when her legs gave.

She steadied herself for a moment as the yellowshirt hooked the *Iho* to his mule. Yes, Beth had broken down and given her Mosquito a name. It didn't feel as right with her as with her Wasps, but sometimes, it was easier to give in than buck tradition. So, there was the name on the prow, her rank and name, her thirteen kills, and now, with twenty missions, another "nickel" would be added to the three already painted on.

At least there was no debrief, as there was after just about every Wasp flight. What mattered was the data gathered by her instruments. She was just a truck driver, hauling the instruments around. And with another dry run, there was nothing she had to report, nor anyone who cared much what she might have noticed.

The data was being analyzed as a matter of course, but for the next eight or ten hours, she was on her own.

A zombie Twister passed her in the corridor, going to her scout.

"Hey, did you hear?" her fellow pilot asked.

"Hear what?"

"You're no longer the Navy's top ace. The Paladin's commander just hit fifteen. Got three in his last mission."

Things had gotten better between Beth and Twister of the last couple of weeks. They weren't besties, but there wasn't the outright antagonism that the other pilot had shown to Beth upon her arrival. Still, there seemed to be more than a bit of glee in her voice as she told Beth.

Beth shrugged, said, "Good for him," then continued on her way. She knew who Commander "Killjoy" Reicher was, of course, and now as a Mosquito pilot, she wasn't adding anything to her tally. It had only been a matter of time before the commander, or any one of the other top aces passed her. But she didn't care. It was all for the good of humanity.

Except she did care. She felt a loss in her heart. She'd been the best, and now, because she was stuck flying Mosquitos, that title had been wrenched from her. She was surprised that she cared as much, thinking she was beyond the ego trip. But there it was.

And suddenly, she didn't want to go back to the galley or their stateroom. She didn't want others, either with understanding compassion or glee, to keep telling her the news.

She took a left down the G corridor, making her way to the ship's company officer's country, then into the hallowed ground of the senior officers. She rang one of the staterooms, and a moment later, Wyma opened the hatch, a smile breaking out on her face when she saw who it was.

"Come on in, Beth," she said, standing back so that Beth could step inside the small sitting room.

Beth still didn't know Wyma's equivalent rank, but the fact that she was in rarified company and that she had a sitting room, even a small one, was evidence enough that she was right on up there.

Given that, and given the fact that they were so different, Beth was still surprised that the two of them had bonded. Wyma was lightyears smarter than Beth, and sometimes, when the woman reverted to science-speak, Beth was lost. Still, she enjoyed Wyma's company more to that of her fellow pilots—not that she would admit that to anyone.

Wyma stepped back to check her display, then asked with a frown, "I didn't see that you ran into anything interesting. Did I miss something?"

Beth had only been back aboard for five minutes, but she should have known that the xenolinguist would have already checked.

"No, no," Beth said, flipping a seat down from the bulkhead and collapsing on it. "I just . . ."

"What, Beth?" Wyma asked when Beth trailed off.

"Just down. And tired."

"As can be expected by your operations tempo."

"And . . . well . . ."

Wyma looked at her expectantly.

"I'm no longer the Navy's top ace!" Beth snapped out, with far more force than she'd intended.

I guess I do care.

"And by becoming a scout, you no longer have a means to regain your position," Wyma said. "And by no longer having this title, you lack the validation you need to prove to yourself that you belong, that you are worthy."

The woman was somewhat socially awkward, but she still understood human nature.

"I know, it's stupid," Beth said. 'But when Twister took such pleasure in telling me that the Paladin's commander is now one up on me, well . . ."

"You do realize that I often feel the same way."

"What? You do? But you're a . . ." she said, waving a hand to indicate the stateroom.

"And I work for others, far more respected than me. I told you my immediate superior is a GT. Well, sixty-four-percent of the people in my field are GTs."

Beth raised her eyebrows at that. The Golden Tribe were the highest of society. Most lived their lives almost separate from the rest of humankind, but some decided to serve in various positions. But for so many to be in alien linguistics? That was odd, but it also explained why Wyma might feel like she had to prove herself. It would be difficult for her to gain reputation and position with so many GTs in her field.

"And that's why you're working so hard to break the code," Beth said.

"And why I am pursuing a little-regarded path," Wyma conceded.

Maybe we aren't so different after all.

Beth yawned and stretched.

"Your reputation is cemented into the public psyche, Beth, and you don't need the be the top ace for validation."

Beth started to say something, but Wyma cut her off. "We can put you on the psychiatrist's couch later and discuss your life if you want, but you look exhausted, Beth. Maybe you should get some rest before your next mission."

Beth said, "I know, but I really don't want to go back to my quarters. I don't want to face the other pilots right now. But I guess I have to."

She stood up to leave, and Wyma said, "Why don't you just use my rack for a bit. Take a nap here, if you want."

Beth glanced over at the rack—no bed, a real bed—in the next room. She wondered if it was as comfortable as it looked.

"No, I couldn't," she forced out.

"Yes, you can," Wyma said, taking Beth by the hand and leading her to the bed. She gave it a pat. "See, it's pretty nice, all things considered."

"But it's your rack."

"I've got work to do. I'll be fine. When's your next mission?"

"I've got about nine hours, unless something's changed."

"You lie down here. I'll wake you in seven hours so you can get some food in you. I'll tell your chief that I'm debriefing you so he knows where to find you if you're needed."

Beth reached out and touched the mattress. She knew she should just go back to her shared stateroom, but . . .

"You're sure I'm not putting you out?"

"Not in the least. I've plenty to do right now."

With a sigh, Beth gave in. She sank down on top of the rack. It was as comfortable as it looked. Within seconds, she was out.

****

Wyma was shaking her awake, and she struggled to reach the surface, her mind numb.

"Wha . . . ? Is it time already?"

"Wake up, Beth."

Beth sat up, her mouth full of cotton and her breath vile.

"OK, I'm up."

She was dead-tired, but after a shower and some chow, she'd be ready.

Wyma was ashen-faced, looking at her, hands on Beth's shoulders.

"What's wrong?" Beth asked.

"Lieutenant Gorman. Twister. She's disappeared."

"No, that's not right. She's on a mission. I saw her on the way back from the hangar."

"No. I mean, on her mission. She shot her gate, and then nothing."

Beth shook her head, trying to clear it. Wyma wasn't making sense. If Twister was in trouble, then she'd tell her guardian angels. Her instruments would still be sending data.

"What about her—"

"Nothing, Beth. Nothing."

If there was nothing, then . . .

Beth swallowed hard. Something had taken Twister out. She was KIA.

Chapter 9

Beth sat in the back of the SCIF, the *Valley Forge's* secure briefing room. What was being discussed affected her, but she didn't say a word. It was taking a while for all of this to sink in.

The meeting was with the top brass back on Earth, and the vice-director himself was chairing it. On the ship's side, the ship's captain, god aboard the *Forge*, was a peon. As this concerned the ship, they were linked into the meeting, but in actuality, after the captain gave her four-minute brief on what she knew about Twister—and that wasn't much—they had all been relegated to observer status.

Beth wasn't even sure why she was at the meeting. Yes, she was a scout pilot, but she was just a boot warrant officer. Whatever her orders were, she'd salute smartly and march on. She half-expected for someone to realize she was still there and tell her to leave.

She was glad to be there, however. The Navy had a habit of treating its sailors like the proverbial mushrooms: fed shit and kept in the dark. But over the last twenty minutes, she'd heard things that were classified so high that they made her ears bleed just to hear them. This was rarified atmosphere for a mere pilot.

The first thing to hit her had been the fact that Twister was not the first pilot lost in the target system. Another scout pilot from the corvette *FS Dillingham* had been lost in much the same way. A flustered rear admiral had to explain to the vice-premier why, given the complete failure of any data, another scout was sent in without additional precautions. The admiral told the worthy that the high command had assumed some sort of catastrophic gate failure—a rare occurrence, but within the realm of possibility.

The *Dillingham* had only one scout on board, so next up was the *Valley Forge*. Technically, a gate could have been set up in the home system to jump to the target, but the Navy and Directorate had set up an elaborate spiderweb of gates in an attempt to keep Earth and other important population centers from being backtracked by the FALs. And within this actively shifting algorithm, the *Valley Forge* had been up next, and Twister got the mission.

A few hours earlier, it would have been Beth's mission, but she tried, only somewhat successfully, to shove that thought out of her mind. And now, with the entire Navy of Humankind under lockdown, if there was another mission, it was going to the *Forge*. Until Rip returned from his present mission, that meant Beth.

And still, no one knew what had splashed Twister. There had been no warning. A few seconds through the gate, then before she could activate her scanners, she was gone.

A civilian was advocating sending the *Forge* itself through a gate, guns blazing, sure that this was a major Crystal system. After a good minute of this, the vice-director cut him off and turned his attention to a full admiral, asking him what he thought about it. The admiral was skilled at deflection, and after a good thirty seconds, Beth didn't know just where he stood.

She could see the vice-director getting a little angry at that, and finally, he cut off the admiral and turned to the pickup.

"Captain Nguyen, it's your ship. Are you ready to jump into the system? What do you Navy types call it? A recon by force?"

"Sir, the *Valley Forge* is ready and eager to enter the system," the captain said without pause.

There were more than a few surprised intakes of breath in the SCIF. The *Valley Forge* was a big, powerful ship, but it was designed to go into combat along with a host of auxiliary vessels. It had been a long time since the Wars of Retribution, but those lessons, buttressed by the loss of capital ships fighting the FALs, had been ingrained into the Navy psyche.

Another civilian jumped in urging caution, and the *Forge* was forgotten again while one after the other, opposing viewpoints were given.

Hell, for all being supposed experts, none of them know what happened.

"What did I miss?" Rip asked, sliding in to stand beside her. He was still in his flight suit, and he reeked of mission-sweat.

She knew he'd come straight from his Mosquito.

"You know about Twister?"

He nodded, his eyes clouding over for a moment.

"Back there, the brass doesn't know anything. Some of them want to send the *Forge* in through a gate to see what's what."

Rip half-snorted as he took in the holo display. "Won't happen. Navy command isn't going to risk a battle cruiser without knowing what we face. It might have just been a gate malfunction."

"She wasn't the first. The *Dillingham* lost a scout in the system the same way. No data. Nothing."

Rip turned away from the holo display and stared at Beth. "Another scout?"

Beth nodded.

"Mother fuck," he hissed, earning him an elbow from a commander standing on the other side of him.

"Well, I guess this isn't a gate problem," he said quietly. "And that means probably you or me."

Beth nodded. No one had specifically said that. Another scout mission hadn't been mentioned by anyone. But she knew that was the only logical course of action. Until they knew what they faced, be it FALs or something else, risking a Mosquito and pilot would be the course of action chosen. And she knew it was the right thing to do.

The question was whether it would be Rip or Beth to face the unknown.

Chapter 10

The question was not whether it would be Rip *or* Beth.

She looked to the next pad where Rip was climbing into his Mosquito. He settled in, glanced up, and gave Beth a wide smile and a thumbs up.

Beth managed to give him a thumbs-up as well, but she was a bundle of nerves, and her smile felt more like a drunken leer.

"You green, ma'am?" one of the Wasp squadron plane captains asked her.

With both of them taking off at the same time, Yanc was getting Rip ready, and the petty officer, whose name never registered with her, was Beth's acting plane captain.

"All green," she said, almost in a squeak. She cleared her throat, then in a deeper, and hopefully calmer voice, repeated the upcheck.

"Good luck, ma'am. Not that you'll need it. And can I say, it's been an honor to launch you."

It was still hard for her to accept that she was something of a hero to the enlisted sailors. Beth turned to look at the petty officer's name tag on his chest.

"Thank you, Petty Officer Grylmor. I appreciate your help."

The sailor blushed, then stepped back and saluted. Beth looked at him in confusion for a moment before it dawned on her. In the rush to be frocked, Beth had never been in a position to be saluted, which was generally not done while underway. This First Class had just rendered her first salute. Tight in the *Iho's* cockpit, she awkwardly brought up her hand and returned the salute.

According to tradition, she should be giving the petty officer a silver uni—a real coin, not a blockchain electronic transfer. Which, of course, she didn't have in her flight suit. Or back in her quarters, for that matter. She'd have to order one from the antique stores that specialized in coins.

I'm going to have to remember to track him down when I get back, she thought as she cut away her salute, banging her elbow on the edge of her fuselage.

If I get back.

She closed her canopy, and the petty officer stepped back. Returning from a mission was something she rarely considered. In some ways she thought she was invincible, that she would always make it back. Oh, there were a few times during a fight—or when trying to shut down a battleship—that she was sure she was going to buy the farm, but not usually when she was getting ready to sally forth.

This was different, however. What the planners had for her and Rip, well, "suicide mission" was an understatement. Some commander had eagerly told them that they each had a thirty percent chance of survival . . . as if that was a good thing.

Frankly, neither Rip nor she thought that was accurate. The idea that they could . . .

Beth shook her head, focusing on the launch. She didn't want to think of the odds, of the calculations that had been made in setting this mission up. Chaos theory didn't have to rear its head in this. A tiny whisper from it, a tiny nudge, and all the vaunted processing power that had gone into this might as well have been done on an abacus.

It was all well and good that the calculations had been made to a zillion sig-figs. But the universe was not a perfect equation.

Salz stood to the side, watching both pilots. He was chewing on a fingernail, his brows scrunched up. He'd had to do more than a few adjustments to the two Mosquito's systems, and he'd argued vociferously that what he was doing broke all sorts of regulations. It took the ship's captain to get the systems tech to comply, and even then, he'd bitched every second of the time while he was making the changes. "Trashing" them, he said.

It was obvious now that he thought the changes wouldn't work. Beth tended to agree with him.

And then it was time. The yellowshirts lifted each Mosquito and guided them to the rails.

"God speed," the captain passed on the flight net.

Beth looked up to the observation bridge high on the hangar bulkhead. The captain and the other brass would be up there, watching the two of them take off. Beth wondered if Wyma was there, too.

She hoped so.

"See you on the flip side," Rip passed on the S2S.

"Roger that."

The connection was still green, but there was a pause before Rip said in a more somber tone, "I'm glad you came over, Beth. You're a good pilot, but I guess that goes without saying."

Beth *wasn't* glad. She belonged in a Wasp, not some sort of space-going cargo sled. But this could very well be the last time she spoke to Rip.

"I'm glad, too. See you when we get back."

The lights on the rail flashed, and Rip was gone.

Beth pulled out her cross and left it on her chest, then resealed her helmet. It was against regs, she knew, but she needed all the help she could get. As her rail started flashing, she kissed the cross through her face shield and whispered a quick "Ava Maria" before she was whipped down the rail and out into the black.

UNKNOWN SPACE

Chapter 11

"Fire Ant, glad to see you made it," a familiar voice said.

"Halo! That you?"

"The one and only."

"So, you just hanging out here?" Beth asked.

Halo laughed, then said, "For the last four hours. I was hoping we'd get you for this, though. We figured we had a thirty-three-percent chance of that."

Beth felt a rush of . . . belonging? This entire operation had been rushed, with very few details promulgated, but if anyone was going to escort her to the final gate, she was glad it was Oscar Flight.

But if they thought there was only a thirty-three percent chance of it being her, then they didn't know that Twister had been lost. Why keep that from them?

"You doing OK?" Ringworm asked.

"Just happy to be here on this fine Navy day," Beth answered.

Tool and even Marmot, only recently returned to flight status, chimed in with greetings.

"Uh, anything you can tell us? All we know is that we were told to come here and wait for a Skeeter."

"Do you know where we are?" Beth asked.

"Not a clue. Everything's on auto with our nav display blacked out," Halo said.

Beth wasn't sure why the tight secrecy. It had only been a little over eight hours since Twister had disappeared, and did anyone think the FALs had spies on the ship?

She thought Oscar Flight had a right to know, but how much could she reveal without getting into trouble?

She laughed out loud at the thought.

So, I think I'm getting back to the ship?

"Something funny?" Halo asked.

Beth hadn't cut the connection.

"Might as well be funny. I'd cry if it wasn't."

"What do you mean?" Marmot cut in.

Beth took a deep breath, then asked, "What are your orders?"

Their orders were probably just as secret as hers—once again, for ridiculous reasons, in her opinion, but Halo didn't hesitate.

"Wait here cutting square circles in space until you, or a Skeeter, that is, arrived, then escort said scout to the next gate. One more transit, then one more gate. Then, we're to wait for an almost immediate return, being ready to capture any data dumps. If it takes longer than forty-five seconds, we're to blow the gate."

There was a pause as if Halo was waiting for her to comment. When she didn't, he asked, "But that's not possible, right? I mean, an immediate return? Not even a Wasp could loop around and shoot back through the gate like that. You're going to be stuck on the other side."

"It won't be me coming through," Beth said.

Beth could swear that she could see the intensity of each of the four connection display lights heighten as the pilots waited for more.

"Let's get going. We've got a timeline to meet. I'll fill you all in along the way."

There was another moment of silence, then Halo said, "You heard her. Unlock the next nav phase."

****

"God speed, Fire Ant," Halo said as Beth allowed her AI to adjust her heading.

"It's Beth."

"Harmony," Halo said.

Beth blinked her surprise and asked, "Harmony? That's your real name?"

The other three laughed . . . too hard. They sounded as stressed as Beth was.

"My folks were Tannisters. All of us kids were named like that," Halo . . . Harmony said.

"No wonder you became a pilot," Beth said. "You needed another name."

"Bingo!" Marmot said before adding, "And I'm Stacilyn."

"Reece," said Ringworm.

Beth waited a moment, then had to prod. "Tool?"

"Anna."

"Well, all of you, thanks for the escort, but this is it. You know your orders."

"This is stupid," Halo—Beth decided that the Oscar Team leader was going to remain "Halo"—said. "For this to work . . ."

He was just repeating what was roiling around in Beth's own thoughts, but she had to be the brave one—or at least sound like she was.

Already, Stacilyn, Reece, and Anna had broken off, making their loops so that any one of them could blow the gate from the moment Beth shot it until the forty-five seconds had passed.

Beth looked at her display. Two minutes and five seconds until she shot the gate. One minute and thirty-five seconds until she . . . she still couldn't believe what she was about to do. Her heart started racing, and nausea threatened to make an appearance.

"Screw it," she muttered, and she took off her neck-cracker, the helmet which was supposed to keep her brain from being fried from enemy energy weapons.

All against Navy regs, of course, but she didn't want to puke, and she really didn't think having the helmet on was going to make a hill of beans difference in what was going to happen. It wasn't as if the helmet's display was going to be useful.

She desperately wanted to take control of the *Iho* again, to veer off. Going into a dogfight, where she had control, was nothing compared to this. She was just a hunk of meat in the Mosquito, along for the ride. There wasn't anything she could do now. She was committed.

With ten seconds left, she passed, "See you all back on the *Forge*. Keep a seat open for me in the galley!"

She received a chorus of replies before they were all cut off, and the *Iho's* cockpit went dark. Completely dark. Her HUD was cut off, as was everything else.

Almost everything. The tiniest bit of power kept several of her passive scanners alive. She had more electrical impulses in her body at the moment.

And that thought filled her with panic. She grabbed her helmet and almost slammed it back on, shielding even her tiny amount of brain activity. It seemed crazy to think that her brainwaves could be picked up, but the science types didn't know the answer to that, and they didn't want to take any chances.

Her pulse raced higher as the *Iho* sped through space, hopefully in the lantern for the gate. But it wasn't this gate that had her worried. It was the other one, the one through which Rip would be emerging. It was her return gate, just as the one she was about to shoot was Rip's.

It was a crazy concept, she knew. Gate placement was never supposed to be an exact science. Ships could always adjust to a gate, after all. And there was always drift within a system as everything rotated around the galactic core.

If the calculations were correct, if the gate drones accurately placed the gates within an error of less than three meters, then Beth and Rip should be able to return to safety.

If.

And that also assumed that running silent would be enough to defeat whatever had splashed Twister and the other pilot, which was no sure thing. It was a theory, nothing more. She and Rip were being used to test that theory.

Twenty-two seconds after shooting the gate, Beth would know.

Twenty-two seconds.

If she missed the gate, there would be no second chances. No powering up the *Iho* and coming around again. And if that happened, her orders were to self-destruct. It wouldn't get that far, however. Whatever got Twister would take that out of her hands.

And that was a relief. She was sure she'd be able to self-destruct, but she really didn't want that at her hands. Her religion still held that suicide was a sin, and while she didn't believe that, why take any chances?

She counted down the time. Without instruments, she had to do it in her head. Closing her eyes, she clutched her silver cross, trying to keep the doubts at bay. She'd rather face a dozen crystal fighters than sit there motionless, with no control over her fate.

She felt it when she shot the gate, despite what the scientists told people. She opened her eyes as she entered another system. At only .54 C, her visuals through the clear canopy worked.

Thousand-twenty-two . . .

Beth wasn't sure what she expected, but there was nothing out of the ordinary. Just another star system among the billions.

Thousand-twenty -one . . . Thousand-twenty . . .

She just hoped that the passive scanners were doing their thing, that they could figure out what was with this system.

Thousand-nineteen . . . thousand-eighteen . . . thousand-seventeen . . .

I'm alive. Probably longer than Twister was.

Thousand-sixteen . . . thousand-fifteen . . .

A calm washed over her, to her surprise. Whatever was going to happen was already in motion.

Thousand-fourteen . . . thousand-thirteen . . .

The inert *Iho* hurtled through the black.

Thousand-twelve . . . thousand-eleven . . .

Beth craned her head. She and Rip had been synchronized, and they should be passing each other now. That had been a concern as well. On opposing, but very tight courses, there was a significant chance they'd collide. At their combined speeds, there would be nothing left but their component atoms.

But she was still breathing. There was no sudden end to the life she'd known for the last thirty-one years.

Thousand-ten . . . thousand-nine . . . thousand-eight . . .

It had been foolish to try and spot Rip, she knew. Still, she peered ahead as if she could see the gate.

"Thousand-seven . . . thousand-six . . . thousand-five . . ." she switched to count out loud.

"Thousand-four . . . thousand-three . . ." she continued, her voice getting louder and higher-pitched.

"Thousand-two . . . thousand-one . . . ZERO!" she almost shouted.

And nothing. She looked back at the system's star, and it hadn't changed. She was still there.

Despair crashed over her, and she closed her eyes, too drained to fight it back. She knew what she had to do. But she needed power to initiate the self-destruct.

Beth hit the power, and the cockpit flickered back to life.

"Fire Ant, you made it!" an excited voice filled her helmet's speakers.

Surprised, Beth looked around. Space around her was black. No system star.

She'd shot the gate.

FS VALLEY FORGE

Chapter 12

The ship was alive with excitement. The system that Rip and Beth had scanned might very well be the FAL home system. It was Crystal, that was certain, and the sheer numbers made that a very real possibility.

When the word leaked out, the ship was placed in lockdown, a full comms blackout. But that didn't stop the crew from wanting action. Given the order, they would have eagerly jumped into the system to take it to the FALs.

Foolish, certainly, but after almost nine months of searching, they'd finally hit paydirt.

Beth wasn't excited. She was angry.

Rigging the two Mosquitos to run silent had been the key to her survival, but not for Rip. He hadn't made it back. The *Iho's* scanners hadn't picked up what happened to him before she shot her gate to safety, so she knew in her heart that he'd missed the gate. Anna had blown it after 45 seconds, but Beth knew Rip would have had already self-destructed.

When Yanc told her that he'd quietly requested that his course be slightly altered to ensure the two Mosquitos wouldn't collide, that confirmed it, at least in her mind. Wyma had tried to build her up, to tell her that Beth was successful because of her intuition, but in this case, it was because Rip had given her the surer shot, lessening his own chances of survival.

After a flurry of backslapping and congratulations that had almost driven Beth crazy, she'd fallen off the map. No one needed a scout pilot anymore when an attack was on the horizon.

"When can I see her?" she asked the yeoman again.

"I'm sorry ma'am," the young sailor said. "She knows you're here. I'm sure it won't be long now."

Four days after returning, she'd had enough and demanded to see the captain. With over 2,000 sailors and Marines onboard, and given what what going on, she wouldn't have been surprised to have been turned down. But she wasn't an ordinary warrant officer, if she was being honest, and she was damned if she wasn't going to use that to get her way.

Except almost two hours after sitting in the outer stateroom, she was still cooling her heels, waiting for her audience. That was doing nothing for her mood.

She wasn't even sure why she was angry, or more specifically, at whom. This was war, and sailors were killed in war. She was angrier at her situation more than anything else, not at any one person, but she couldn't yell at a situation. Just the night before, she'd snapped at Wyma as her friend asked again if there was anything she observed while in the FAL system that hadn't been picked up by her scanners.

Finally, the hatch to the captain's stateroom opened, and several senior officers filed out. The captain started to go back in when the yeoman said, "Ma'am? Warrant Officer Dalisay?"

The captain looked at Beth, then turned to look back inside her stateroom. She hesitated, then said, "OK, Dalisay. You've got five minutes."

Beth jumped to her feet and followed the captain inside.

A space-going captain might as well be a god, and her stateroom reflected that. The main room was huge, with a conference table big enough for twenty in the center. There was what looked to be a small galley in the back, and two closed hatches led to what were probably her bedroom and a head.

Beth barely let that sink in as she took one of the two seats on the other side of a large, but utilitarian desk. The captain didn't sit behind the desk, but half-sat on the front corner, a sure sign that she was not going to give Beth much time.

"I never really had time to talk to you after you returned aboard," she said.

Which was an understatement. She had met Beth in the hangar . . . or more accurately, she'd met the *Iho* and watched as the memories of the scanners were removed. The data had already been uploaded to the ship and probably half-a-dozen other places as well, but the physical memories could still offer additional information.

"But you did an amazing job. Great work."

"I didn't do anything, ma'am. I just rode a dead stick."

The captain frowned and said, "Still. What you did was above and beyond, and the results, well, I don't have to tell you what they mean to us. I know you'll be commended for the mission."

"I don't care about that," she snapped before shutting her mouth. She had to watch herself, she knew. Frustration was boiling over, and she didn't want to piss off the one person who might be able to help.

The captain looked at her for a long moment, her brows scrunched as she considered Beth before asking, "So, what do you want to see me about?"

"We're going to attack the FALs," she said.

The captain's eyes narrowed slightly, and she said, "Nothing's been decided, Warrant Officer. We don't even know if that was a Crystal system."

Right. Like anyone doubts that.

"Either now or later, we'll be taking it to them, ma'am."

"And if we do?"

"I'm not a scout pilot."

"I would beg to differ, warrant officer. It seems that you've proven yourself as one."

"Any idiot can ride a Skeeter."

Which wasn't exactly true, but Beth was convinced of her main point.

"And . . . ?"

"I'm a fighter pilot, ma'am, and a damned good one. I need to be in the cockpit of a Wasp, not a fuc . . . not a Mosquito. No insult intended to Skeeter pilots. Rip . . . Lieutenant Commander a'Dat was one of the best."

"May he rest in peace," the captain said automatically.

"You don't need me here."

"Last I looked, you're my only scout onboard right now."

"But the *Forge* is in lockdown. There won't be any missions for the near term, not while a major operation is being put together. And by that time, you'll be restocked with everything, including a scout detachment."

"So, what exactly are you trying to say, Dalisay?"

"I want you to put me in a Wasp. Either here or back with the Stingers."

SIERRA STATION

Chapter 13

"Satan's balls, look what the fucking cat dragged in."

"What? you have a cat," Beth asked, momentarily confused before Mercy erupted from her rack and enveloped her sister-in-law.

"Forget it. Just another saying, sista! But what the hell are you doing here?"

"Finished my mission, that's what," Beth said as she could feel her blood pressure drop by the second.

She was home, where she belonged.

"We got word you were gone for good," Mercy said, finally releasing her stranglehold on Beth.

"Things change, you know. The Navy and all."

"Ain't that the truth. But really. You were gone. We've got a new pilot in Fox Flight."

Beth stepped back in surprise. She'd been replaced? A hole opened up in her heart, one that had only been filled upon her return.

Then she realized that of course, she'd been replaced. The squadron didn't just stop because Beth was gone. The Navy wasn't going to leave a gap in the squadron.

Beth was just lucky that she was back here. The best she'd hoped for was to join VF-82 aboard the *Forge*, but the captain had done some heavy politicking for her, and she'd gotten her orders to the scout detachment canceled, which meant she went back to her permanent unit.

"So, what the hell did you do? Where did you go?"

Beth hesitated a moment, then said, "Nothing much. Lots of missions, but nothing exciting. My temp duty orders were canceled, that's all."

Beth was a lousy liar, and she was sure Mercy would see through her, but she'd been warned about telling anyone what had happened. They'd find out soon enough, but for now, she was to keep quiet, and she was going to adhere to that. She didn't want anything to jeopardize being back with the Stingers.

"So, who replaced me?"

Mercy scowled and then said, "Some boot third class. Can't fly worth shit, you know. I thought we were supposed to only get the best here."

Beth held back a smile. Mercy wouldn't be Mercy is she wasn't bitching. And the days of the Stingers being an elite unit were fading away as more and more squadrons were being stood up during the surge. Experienced pilots were being spread out to maximize the overall readiness of the fighter force.

"I'm back, so you have the best," she said.

Mercy huffed and said, "Eat me."

"Good to see you, too."

Mercy picked up Beth's seabag and tossed it on the upper rack. "You're lucky I didn't let anyone else move in."

"Seems to me that as the senior officer here, I should get my choice," Beth said without being serious. She really didn't care.

"Ain't gonna happen. You may be a double-u-oh, but you're still a boot to me."

Chapter 14

"She do OK?" Josh asked, pushing up the ladder so Beth didn't have to jump down.

"Just fine. Like old times."

"Sorry there're no more Novembers for you," her plane captain said.

"The *Tala's* served me well for a couple of years. She still will."

"Still, you should have gotten a November."

"What, and pull one of the pilots assigned to a flight out of theirs?"

Josh scowled and muttered something under his breath as Beth climbed down to the deck.

Beth had been a little put out herself when the CO had told her there were no more Novembers available for her. The squadron was at full T/O, and there weren't enough of the latest and greatest Wasps in the Navy to give a squadron extras. So, Beth had gone from one of the first pilots to get a November to being relegated back to the X-rays.

It turned out OK, however. Her old Wasp, *Seven-six-ninety-two*, had not been sent back yet, so she'd been assigned it instead. Yes, she'd rather have the newer version, but if she had to have an older model, better it be the frame she'd flown so many times. It had served her well before, and she was sure it would again.

In line with naval tradition/superstition, the "*Tala*" had already been taken off the nose when Beth had been assigned that first November, but her name and kills were still there. Beth was tempted to get her five nickels added, but that might stray into too-much-information territory. Josh, who'd been assigned to the pool, was pulled back to be her plane captain, and he'd replaced the *"Tala"* above the rest before her first shakedown.

Beth took a moment to look around the hangar. It was a hub of activity, and the choreographed chaos never ceased to amaze her. She wondered, however, how many people knew what was going on. Most of them were just looking forward to the deployment. A combat deployment for sure, but they didn't know that a FAL system, maybe their homeworld, would be in the Navy's crosshairs.

The CO probably knew, if Beth could read into what seemed to be a more focused approach to her, but who else? Anyone?

In many ways, much of the group dynamics now bypassed Beth. She was with the squadron, but not in a flight. She wasn't even on the T/O. The CO never asked her what she'd done on the *Valley Forge*, and she'd never questioned having an extra pilot on hand. She'd assigned Beth as the squadron assistant admin officer, where her only job, the best she could tell, was to ensure that every sailor had a will or living trust. It wasn't a flying billet, but with the old *Tala* still on the station, she'd told Beth to get it recertified.

Beth understood. She was on the bench, getting ready to step up. Even without the upcoming operation, chances were that one of the other pilots would either get splashed or taken off flight status during the course of the deployment. Beth would be there to fill in when that happened.

She wished she was still with Mercy in Fox Flight, but this was better than not flying at all.

FS YALU RIVER

Chapter 15

"So, you just went and had them removed?"

"Harvested, sista. That's the word."

Beth rolled her eyes. "They took out your eggs. Eight hours before we deployed, you went down to Refuge, found a civilian doctor, and had them *harvested*?"

"Yeah, that's about right." She touched the sides of her belly, then flipped her thumbs outward in a quick motion. "Babing. Out they came, into a cyrovac tube, and off to New Cebu and Rock."

"You could have at least told me," Beth said, feeling left out of the process.

"Why, so you could have come down and held my hand?"

"Well, no . . ."

Without a flying billet, the CO had started loading more secondary duties on her—were they still secondary when there were at least ten of them now on her official list of duties? While the pilots only had to worry about their personal gear and fighters, Beth now had over 200 others in the squadron and tons of gear that she had to load out.

Beth hadn't often thought of the sailors who weren't directly involved with flying to keeping the fighters combat-ready, but she'd just had a master class in all that they did to keep the squadron functioning. And one thing was for sure: even if she'd wanted to, there'd been no way she could have sneaked down to the planet while Mercy had her eggs harvested.

"So, all I did was keep you from worrying," Mercy said, as if that ended the matter.

"You could have missed movement," Beth said, not willing to give up.

"Then you'd have yourself a November, right?"

Beth stared daggers at her sister-in-law, who said, "Oh, too sensitive?"

Mercy knew that Beth was disappointed in not being assigned to a flight, and Beth thought that was both a low blow and, at the same time, minimizing the risk Mercy had taken by going down to the planet. Desertion in wartime was a serious offense, even if it was not done on purpose.

This really means a lot to her, Beth told herself. *Don't be upset with her.*

"How much did it cost?" she asked, not really mollified, but trying not to take it personally.

"Almost four grand," Mercy said as if it was nothing.

"What? Four-freaking-grand? Mercy, that's a lot of unis!"

"What else was I going to do with it for the next who-knows-how-long? Besides, Rock knows. I had to cut his allotment, but we agreed."

"You know, you could have waited. The Naval Hospital would have done it for free."

"And how long until this fucking war is over? Huh?" Mercy snapped, breaking her complacent facade. "And that's if I even make it back alive."

Mercy hadn't mentioned her premonitions of her death since Beth returned from the *Forge*, but it was now evident that her belief she was going to die was still there.

"Nothing's going to happen to you," Beth told her, sitting down on Mercy's rack and putting her arm around her. "You're too ornery to let the FALs get you."

Mercy stiffened, then almost melted into Beth's arm, putting her head on her best friend's shoulder. "I hope the FALs know that," she said in a quiet voice.

Being aboard the ship didn't mean Beth now had a lot of free time. Her to-do list was a kilometer long as the squadron settled in, but for the moment, Mercy needed her, and a pilot never abandoned a wingman.

Chapter 16

"I swear, we had them last week," Lieutenant Max Waldorf said, running his hand through hair that probably was over regulation length.

"Then they would be here, Lieutenant," Beth said.

Beth wouldn't know what a decspan wrench was if it fell and hit her on her head, and she'd wished she'd never heard of one. But the weekly inventory was short by three. Either their RFID chips were down, which seemed like too much of a coincidence, or they'd been disabled and the wrenches taken.

Beth, being the squadron shitty job officer, had the unenviable duty of conducting a physical inventory of the four maintenance spaces to try and find them. And as she didn't know what they were, she needed the lieutenant and the chief to help out.

At fourteen-thousand, five-hundred-and-three unis as their stated value, that was almost half of the lieutenant's annual salary.

It's not like they could have been taken off the ship. The planned port call at Hobsons, which was to be the last time to resupply before the deployment started in earnest, had been canceled. Beth was probably one of the few people aboard the ship who knew the real reason that happened. Not the only one. The commodore was spending most of his time in his stateroom with other senior officers, and the crew was gradually becoming aware that something was up. But no one knew the specifics.

Beth knew.

That didn't matter at the moment, however. Attacking the Crystal homeworld, if that was what they'd discovered, or not, she still had to do this inventory. If they didn't find the wrenches, the lieutenant could be on the hook for them.

"Sir, if we can just start pulling everything out, we can begin. I hope they show up."

The maintenance officer shook his head and muttered under his breath before turning and saying, "Chief, I guess we need to start. I want all hands on this. I swear, if one of these yahoos . . ."

Whatever he was going to do to "these yahoos" was lost as the announcement over the IMC said, "All hands, all hands, the *FS Yalu River* is on full communications blackout. All scheduled morale and welfare calls are canceled until further notice. I repeat, all scheduled morale and welfare calls aboard the *FS Yalu River* are canceled until further notice. Stand by for a message from the commodore at seventeen hundred hours ship time."

There were several dismayed shouts as they heard the news. Sailors had to normally wait up to a week to get a comms slot to call back home.

Beth checked the time. Twenty-two minutes until the commodore's message.

"I think we can stop this for now, Lieutenant."

"No, I want to take care of this. I can't afford another fuck-up."

Behind him, the chief narrowed his eyes ever-so-slightly. The lieutenant's reputation in the squadron was not great, and from the chief's reaction, that reputation might be deserved.

But Beth would bet a month's pay that she knew what the commodore was going to say, and she thought that in twenty-two minutes, no one was going to be concerned about three missing wrenches.

Chapter 17

Beth would have won the bet . . . probably. It would have depended on the exact terms. Yes, the commodore broke the news to the twelve ships in the task force. They had a target.

But this wasn't going to be the all-out show of force that Beth had expected. Six task forces, twenty-two percent of the Navy's capital ships, were going to converge on the system. The rest of the fleet would be standing by, both protecting Earth and the rest of the core worlds and forming a large reserve force.

This was the conservative approach, something the vast majority of pilots thought was the wrong way to go about it. If the system was, in fact, the FAL homeworld, then it needed to be hit with the full force of the Navy of Humankind, not some sort of reconnaissance-in-force.

But the science-types were not even in full agreement that this was the FAL homeworld. It was big, that was for certain, the densest gathering of Crystals ever observed. But the homeworld? There was no way to know for certain given the observed facts. And it was that uncertainty that was the deciding factor. Humans had to know more, and they couldn't get that by drones or sending other shut-down scouts flitting around the edges of the system.

The combined task force, under command of a full Admiral, was not going in light-handed, however. Three unmanned monitors, stripped down of all weapons and now nothing more than armored sleds, were rigged to become the most powerful weapon ever unleashed by humanity. The rest of the task force's mission was to get those weapons to the target. Homeworld or not, it was going to be reduced to nothing. Whatever FALs were there would never be a threat to humanity again.

"You green?" Josh asked her.

She gave him a thumbs up. Beth was not with the squadron's sixteen flights, but she was not going to ride this out inside the *Yalu River*. She was going to be a picket, guarding the task force's gate. Her only mission was to destroy the gate if necessary. And she had a backup. The *FS Springbok* was not going to jump the gate, staying on the near side, and someone on the bridge would be ready to destroy it if it came to that.

Beth felt the familiar thrill start to build within her, something she'd missed with flying her Mosquito. With all respect due to Rip and Twister, she didn't like being a scout, and she was at a loss as to how other scouts, who had all been Wasp pilots first, did it.

But now, as the *Tala* hummed with power, she was ready. This was what she was born to do.

The *Tala* settled into the lock, and a few moments later, she was shot into space. It wasn't until the Tala's FC engines kicked in, however, that she exhaled. She was finally flying again.

Alone, though, which felt weird. Wasps were flown in flights, not as a singleton. But it still felt good. She ran a quick check, then let her AI take over, shooting her through four successive gates until there was only one more, the one that would return her to the system.

Beth had been the only human to be in over fifty systems, back when she was a commercial pilot, searching for exploitable worlds. At the moment, she was still the only human alive who'd been in the target system.

At the moment.

She checked her timer. In less than half-an-hour, over a hundred-thousand humans would make their uninvited appearance. This was history in the making. Beth wished that she was at the tip of the spear, but at least she'd be there.

But for now, it was just waiting. She didn't even have control of the *Tala*. With so many ships, large and small, in the invasion fleet, where timing was critical in getting the force through six gates, the complexity was too much to rely on humans. The traffic control AIs would send the ships through. Beth would be the second-to-last one through but still be only three seconds after the first unmanned monitors shot the gate to clear the way for the rest of the task force.

Beth watched her HUD closely, her excitement rising. She gave a loud "Get some" when the monitors hit all three gates—and didn't feel stupid that she was encouraging unmanned ships. They were still part of humankind, and if they could help crush the threat, then she'd be happy to thank their electronic brains.

Before she knew it, the *Tala* shot the gate, not into a holovid maelstrom, but into the calm before the storm. Four of the monitors were knocked out, and it looked as if some of the manned craft had seen some action, but for the most part, the task force was a mass of humanity's might, sweeping on six fronts. They looked unstoppable.

Beth wanted to watch for a moment, but she was now in control of her Wasp, and she had her own mission. She pulled the *Tala* around in a tight loop, slowing down until she faced her gate. She powered up the GDS that had been attached to her Wasp, taking the place of her torpedo pods.

Now it was waiting, waiting for the order she hoped she would never receive.

****

"Initiate destruction sequence of Gate K-L-five-four-one-one," the voice came over her speakers on a Priority 1 override.

"Hell," Beth muttered, her heart heavy.

It had been pretty obvious to her, over the last two hours, that it would come to this. What had started out in such a grand and glorious manner had devolved into a rout.

The first lines of FAL defenses had crumbled in the face of the assault, but as humanity had closed in, more and more FAL craft had rushed to meet them. Unknown weapons had reached out from seemingly empty space. The *FS Titan* had been the first capital ship to fall, blasted out of space by something very fast and powerful. Over four thousand souls, gone in an instant.

Sitting out at the edge of the system, Beth was not on any of the command nets, so she didn't have a good grasp of the fight, but she could observe the human ships, and she could see what was happening. After the *Titan*, two more battleships were hit, one after the other, and then one of the sleds with the planet busters.

Each ship winking out was a dagger to her heart. Sailors were dying out there.

Beth adjusted her filter to the Stingers, wishing she could listen in. They were in intense combat with FAL fighters, and while it looked like they were dishing out more than they were receiving, the fact of the matter was that there were always more FALs joining the fight.

She wanted to call Mercy, hoping that she was still in the fight, but she knew any interruption could spell doom.

The *Yalu River* was hit, but still, her guns were working, reaching out to sweep FALs from space. Then the second sled was taken down, still thirty minutes from deployment range. One was left, but it would only take one to turn the battle.

Eight minutes before weapons deployment, the last sled was destroyed. Without the sled, without the battleships and cruisers, the mission was a failure. A general recall was sounded.

But the FALs were not going to let the humans just leave the field of battle. More swarmed from the planet and two of the moons, and the surviving Wasps started to form a rearguard, enabling others to run for the gates.

"Mercy, please make it back," Beth prayed as she checked her GDS. She hadn't wanted to use it, but the writing was on the wall.

Within an hour, the first ships and fighters started to stream past Beth and through the gates. Beth couldn't tell for sure, but it looked like some of the fighters were being grappled by others.

She broke comms once, calling Mercy on the S2S, but there was no answer. Mercy had told Beth she wasn't going to make it through the battle, and Beth was only now coming to grips with the fact that her sister-in-law may have been right.

Tears formed and started running down her cheeks, and she had to shake free of the grip of grief. There would be time later to mourn if Mercy didn't make it back, but she still had a mission. She watched the leading edge of the wave of FAL ships approach, and she knew the order would come soon.

And now it had.

"Acknowledge, Yankee-Two-Two-Six," the voice insisted, the calm demeanor showing the slightest of cracks.

There were still too many friendlies still on this side of the gate. She could program her AI to figure out how many—and who—were still in the system, but she didn't have time.

"Roger, understood," Beth passed. "Initiating sequence."

Beth was tempted to ask for another thirty seconds, but she knew if she balked, then the unknown sailor on the *Springbok* would take over.

Her mind was racing. What she was about to do would strand fellow sailors, sentencing them to death. But orders were orders, and she understood the imperative.

Ships were still passing her, heading for safety, some of the fighters accelerating at speeds that were only possible with G-shot. None of the capital ships, though. The *Yalu River* was still on her display, but it was dead in space, drifting. If anyone was still alive on her, they were about to be stranded.

"Hurry, guys. Get the hell out of here," she said aloud as she started the sequence.

She deployed the GDS, which was composed of three parts: a "hook," a molecular disintegrator, and an explosive charge.

Whether this was the actual FAL home system or not, it was imperative that not a trace of a gate be left. Unlike previous engagements, this meant that a fighter standing off on the other side and firing at the gate would be good enough. This new system had been in development for close to seven months, but this would be the first time it would be used in combat . . . here and at the other five gates as well.

Beth was going to fly back through the gate, towing the GDS at the end of a ten-kilometer line. The hook was just that. Electronic fingers would reach out and snag the physical structure of the gate, all four kilos of it. That would start the gate folding in on itself, almost pulling the edges themselves through the active gate. A picosecond later, an omnidirectional impulse detonator would set off the disintegrator field in the gate, a field that would eat away at the very molecules that made it. Theoretically, the molecules would continue their motion, folding in on themselves and through to the other side, like an inverted sock. The final component was the charge, a small, powerful nuke that would scatter whatever traces were left on the far side. Theoretically, there wouldn't be a single atom left on the FAL side, nothing they could use to reverse engineer the human gate system.

The GDS fully deployed, and Beth ran a quick check. All was green.

A larger ship passed by, but Beth couldn't take the time to ask her AI to identify it. It didn't matter which one it was, only that more sailors were going to survive.

The *Tala* was already oriented to the gate, just a few short kiloklicks ahead. Once she engaged her drive, it would take approximately fifteen seconds for her to pass through, towing the GDS. Fifteen seconds and the escape route for any other survivors would be cut off.

Beth crossed her self and put the *Tala* in motion. Her compensators hummed to keep her alive as power coursed through the Wasp, shooting it forward.

"Mercy, you out there, sista?" she sent on the S2S one last time

There was no reply, and with a sob, Beth shot the gate. A picosecond later, the gate was no more.

BOLLINGTON STATION

Chapter 18

Beth jumped down to the hangar deck. The place was a madhouse. Bollington Station was not big enough for the fighters and smaller craft that were landing, even if the numbers had been more than halved during the battle. But with the *Yalu River* lost, all of the surviving Wasps from the Stingers and Harpies, needed a place to land. And now, it was pure chaos and the limited number of yellowshirts, aided by green and purpleshirts, were trying to get fighters and other craft off the pads and out of the way so more could land.

The retreat from the FAL homeworld had been chaotic, to say the least. The Navy had prepared for something like this, but the plan had not been promulgated well. Beth didn't think that anyone expected the severity of the defeat.

Beth had shot the gate, destroying it with her passage, then shot the next gate as assigned. But the *Yalu River* was gone. The fighters didn't have a platform there with which to rendezvous.

The wounded were evacuated first, but the remaining ships and fighters from their task force staged in the sector for over five hours before they received orders. Beth, along with the survivors of the two squadrons that had been aboard the *Yalu River*, were given the order to proceed to Bollington Station.

"Where are we supposed to go?" Beth asked a yellowshirt.

"I don't know, ma'am, but you can't stay here," the petty officer said.

Beth looked around, hoping to spot Mercy. She saw Bull from across the hangar, and a few of the other Stinger pilots, but no shock of bright red hair.

"Please, ma'am. All pilots are to leave the hangar," a yeoman came up to her and said.

"But to where?"

"Right now, in the main galley. Just follow the purple line," the yeoman said, pointing to a door leading out of the hangar spaces.

Beth wanted to argue, but if they were gathering in the galley, that would be the best place to find the others. She left the hangar and followed the purple guideline. Sailors were milling about, but there was a general movement forward.

She spotted Petty Officer Addad, the boot pilot Mercy had told her about, up ahead, and pushed her way through to him.

"Where's Mercy?" she demanded.

"I don't know. She was hit just before the recall."

"You don't know where your flight leader is?" Beth asked, taking him by the collar of his flight suit and hauling him down to her level.

"She was ordered back, and Wingnut took over. I didn't see her," he protested.

Beth let him go. The idiot didn't know a thing. She pushed forward, using her low center of gravity to barge through.

The Bollington Station main galley was huge, but it was rapidly filling up with sailors—no Marines, she noted. They'd have all been on the larger capital ships, which had taken the bulk of the losses.

There were a lot of sailors filling the space, but, at the same time, not enough. Beth didn't know if all of the *Yalu*

River's 18,000-person mini-task force had been ordered to Bollington Station, but she doubted there were 2,000 people crowding inside the galley. Lots of pilot suits, but she could see the shoulder flashes of several of the smaller capital ships.

And that was for only a sixth of the entire Task Force Gauntlet. From what Beth saw, the losses were as bad with the other five elements.

Beth didn't want to contemplate the magnitude of the disaster at the moment. She was more interested in if Mercy, if Josh . . .

"Oh, fuck!" she said, stopping dead in her tracks.

The *Yalu River* had been lost, and Josh had been aboard. Somehow, with everything else going on, that hadn't dawned on her.

Tears started rolling down her cheeks. Josh!

"Keep moving," someone said from behind her, giving her a push.

Like a zombie, she tottered forward until she could move to the side of the galley, out of the way.

Josh had been her first plane captain, a young spaceman, sent to her so she would be senior to him. She'd considered sending him back until the young man had proven himself. He was the best, and until now, Beth hadn't even realized that he was gone. Guilt washed over her. This was Josh!

She put her back against the bulkhead and closed her eyes. Tens of thousands of lives had been lost during the battle, and Josh was just one of them, she knew. That didn't make the pain any less.

Eventually, the flow petered out. The blowers struggled to keep the air quality up with so many aboard, but Beth didn't care. Josh was gone. Probably Mercy, too. She'd lost friends before. She'd lost Commander Tuominen. But the cost of the war had just crossed a line with her. She was heartbroken, but also angry.

The vidscreens on all the bulkheads came on, revealing a full admiral. "Sailors of Task Force Gauntlet, you have suffered a grievous loss,"

Boos and hisses rose to greet him.

"I know that it's hard to hear, but the truth is the truth. No one blames you. You did your duty with courage and honor, but your mission was untenable," he almost spat, his anger obvious.

"We follow the orders of our civilian leadership, as we did for the operation. Once we expressed our concern, we saluted and marched on. That is the way it's done."

From the look on his face, this admiral didn't agree with that. Beth wondered who he was. She knew admirals who'd been pilots, but not many more fleetwide.

"But I want to give you my oath, THAT-WILL-NOT-HAPPEN-AGAIN!" he thundered, his face turning red with rage.

"We're going back to the Fucking Aliens homeworld, but this time, the Navy will dictate the terms. We will go in full force, using the entire might of the Navy. No hunk of damned crystal is going to be able to stand in our way, because we're the damned Navy of Humankind, the greatest force ever assembled!"

There were cheers now from the gathered sailors. They'd been bloodied, they'd lost shipmates, and they wanted revenge. And if the admiral was right, this time, they wouldn't go in on the cheap. They'd go in with enough force to overwhelm the FALs.

Beth found herself lifted, and she cheered with the rest as the admiral railed on. She wanted to destroy the FALs, and he was promising her the means to do it.

The admiral calmed down somewhat and told them that the Navy was going to rebuild the losses, and it was up to every one of them to pull more than their weight to further the cause.

If they just trusted their leadership and put all their effort into the rebuilding, nothing could stand in their way.

The cynical among them might see this as posturing by Navy HQ, but something in the man seemed genuine, and Beth believed his sincerity. The question was if he had the power to make his promises good.

After he finished, another voice came over the 1MC, starting the task of making some order out of the mass of battle survivors. Pilots were directed back to the hangar, others to various spaces aboard the station.

Beth joined the rest of the pilots. Her heart was heavy, but there were the flickering sparks of revenge, just seeking the means to explode into a raging fire.

She spotted the XO ahead of her and started to push forward. She was going to demand a November Wasp and a place with a flight when steel-bound arms wrapped around her, stopping her cold.

"Satan's balls, sista, I didn't think you'd made it!"

Beth twisted around to the sight she most longed to see.

Mercy was crying, and Beth joined in as she hugged her in a death grip.

"I thought you didn't make it, either. Addad said that you were hit."

"He made it, too! Thank God. Yeah, I was hit. Took out my comms, my targeting AI, but the *Touhi* got me back in one piece."

"Josh didn't make it. He was on the *Yalu*."

"Yeah, Porter, too," Mercy said, her smile fading.

"I'm going to miss him," Beth said. "But I'm just am so glad to see you. I couldn't have borne it if . . ."

"I know, I know. Me, too. So, now what?' Mercy said, looking around at the other pilots as they passed them in the passageway.

"You heard the admiral, sista. Now we go back, but this time do it right and kick some FAL butt!"

Beth stood up, her heart racing.

The CO looked at the four pilots from Fox Flight and said, "That means you, too!"

"What's going on?" Mercy asked.

"The FALs have invaded the home system!" the CO yelled over her shoulder as she ran out of the office.

Chapter 20

Twenty-six minutes after receiving the word, Beth was back in the *Tala*, heading for the first gate. Fox flight had no specific mission yet, but she'd been assured she'd have one before jumping into the home system.

The Omega Contingency, the ever-evolving plan to protect the home system and some of the other key systems, had been implemented for the first time in history.

Calling it a plan was not really accurate. It was more of a series of contingent plans that could be collated into a working defense in a short amount of time, with units being plugged in the best they could.

"What do you think?" Mercy asked.

"I don't know," Beth answered, and she truly didn't know what to think.

The last twenty-six minutes had been a blur of rote chaos. Their training kicked in, and there had been little time to let the ramifications sink in. Now, that they had another twelve minutes before their first jump, it hit her.

The home system was under attack. She didn't know by how many FALs, or where they were at the moment, but the *home system*!

Beth was from New Cebu, a backwater planet out on the spiral arm. She'd only been to Earth twice, both times for Navy PR, and it wasn't even the most populated system in the galaxy, but it was still the ancestral home of humanity. The emotional impact was like a kick in the gut.

She felt nauseous, so she absentmindedly took a sip . . . and was surprised when she tasted ice-cold Coke. Somehow, in the rush to get the *Tala* launched again, Moid had managed to restock the Number 6 reservoir.

One of the other plane captains had told Moid that Josh had always kept Beth in Coke, despite regulations. Moid had decided to keep the tradition going. Stupid and inconsequential, but the fizzy liquid brought a note of reality, snapping her mind back to her job, which was to make sure her flight was ready.

She took a deep breath, burped, then said, "Fox Flight, this is it. We'll be shooting the gate in . . . in eleven minutes and thirty-two seconds. We'll be under vector control, so I don't know when the next jump will be, but it should take us right to the home system.

"No use hiding where we're jumping from now," Mercy said.

Beth tried to pick up any anxiety in her sister-in-law's voice, but for someone who'd been on edge for the last several months, she seemed in control, the old Mercy back.

"Right. We don't have a mission yet, but I expect we'll get it at Lexon before we shoot the next gate."

Lexon, where as an Hamdani Brothers' explorer pilot, she'd headed out to sixty-four worlds. The circle was closing.

Which was not much of a coincidence. The *Jungle* had been out in the nether spaces, far from anywhere and certainly without a direct gate to the home system. Lexon had been a central nexus point, with over twenty permanent gates.

"What if we don't get our mission," Grape asked. "What do we do then?"

"Then, we adjust and adapt. If FALs are in the system, we kill them. Understand?" Beth said with a little more force than she'd intended.

I should be calming him, not pushing up the stress levels.

"For the moment, just run through your diagnostics again."

Which wasn't going to do much. Nothing short of a full-on shut-down was going to keep any of them from jumping to the home system. But if the other three pilots were running through the manual checklist, then they wouldn't be getting stressed about what was going to come.

Me, too, she thought belatedly.

She started the checklist, watching her HUD as each system logged in green. The

The *Tala* was purring like a kitten. She hadn't really bonded with Moid—the Coke was a good start, however—but he seemed capable. With essentially no turn-around, the Wasp was still ready for battle.

She paid particular attention to her weapons readouts. The November Wasp carried five torpedoes instead of the older version's three. With the torpedoes the most effective weapon against the Crystal ships, that gave the flight a significantly bigger punch.

The other weapons were not ignored. Her P-18 was running green, and the railgun was loaded with 8,110 depleted uranium rounds. Between the three, the *Tala* had more actual firepower than early space-going battleships.

The last check was her fireturds. The heat control system had gone through a number of upgrades, but the basic concept was the same. The heat buildup in the Wasp was transferred to molypendium billets that were then ejected into space. The system worked better than the early attempts, and other than breaking a Wasp's cloaking, they worked well now, but it was the Navy way to check and recheck everything.

"Beth," Mercy passed on the S2S.

"You finished with your checklist?" Beth asked, looking at the readouts from the Louhi. They hadn't flashed green.

"Not yet."

"What are you waiting for, sista? We shoot the gate in less than seven minutes."

"I just . . . well, if something happens to me, I want you to promise—"

"That's enough of that, Mercy!" Beth said with some venom. Evidently, the "old" Mercy wasn't back after all, and Beth was getting more than a little tired of her sister-in-law's doom-and-gloom.

"I feel it, Beth," she said in a plaintive voice.

"Yeah, and you felt it last time, too. But you made it back when so many others didn't."

"Barely. I lost my weapons and comms. A few more seconds, and who knows?"

Beth took a few deep breaths, then in a calm voice, said, "Barely still means you made it back. No G-shot, nothing."

"I know, but I can't drop the feeling. I think this one is it."

Beth rolled her eyes. She'd flown with Mercy for most of her still short career as a pilot, but maybe it would be better to fly on separate flights from now on.

"You can feel all you want. We've got a mission here, and I need you to get your head out of your ass and pilot," she snapped.

There was a pause, then a simple, "Aye-aye, ma'am," before Mercy cut the S2S.

Beth felt bad, getting on Mercy's case like that, but Earth was being attacked, and she didn't have time to deal with Mercy's premonitions. The fate of humankind hung in the balance.

One by one, Mercy's checklist went green. Beth thought about saying something more but decided to leave it alone.

A few minutes after Mercy finished, the flight shot the gate into Lexon Central. Going through a gate anywhere was the same as anywhere else. There were no landmarks, per se, and while a Wasp's AI could immediately pinpoint the fighter by looking at the stars, Beth couldn't. Lexon had been her home for years, but there was no pull. It was just a waystation for her now.

Her incoming alerted, and Beth immediately opened it. As expected, it contained their mission. She took a quick look while her AI plotted their course once through the next gate.

The home system had been invaded by thousands of FAL ships, and more were appearing out beyond Neptune's orbital plane. Contact with the Home Guard had already been initiated, with the FALs sweeping through their opposition.

The big picture was almost overwhelming, and Beth had to force herself to look beyond it and to Fox Flight's little slice of the action. She scrolled to Paragraph 3, then interfaced to visuals.

"Fox Flight, we have a mission."

The four Wasps were not joining the core defenses surrounding Earth and Mars. They were not part of the defense of Titan or Ganymede. Out past Neptune, out past Pluto, was SRR-1004, a small but important cog in the system web.

Fox Flight's mission was to protect it.

HOME SYSTEM

Chapter 21

Fox Flight jumped into a chaotic home system. It was difficult not to try to take in the scope of the maelstrom, but they had a mission, and that came first.

The course to their target was downloaded from one of the huge defense AIs the instant they hit the system, and Beth uploaded it to the other three pilots. The home system had hundreds of gates, so they were able to shoot close, and nineteen minutes later, the flight reached SRR-1004, moving into a clover formation, which gave wide coverage and allowed all of the Wasps to quickly orient on any given threat.

This far out, Sol was a small, bright disk. It didn't look like much, but it had given life to humanity. Would the home system survive the day?

In position, and with no FALs close, Beth took the opportunity to shift to some of the other bands to see what was happening.

It was sobering. The FALs had jumped farther out then she'd expected, closer to the orbits of Neptune and Jupiter. At the moment Earth, Luna, and Mars were not under direct attack . . . but with the numbers of FALs still appearing, Beth didn't think that would last. The entire Navy and Home Guard, even if joined by the other various planetary guards and semi-criminal fleets in the far reaches, couldn't match the numbers of FALs in the system.

And as she watched, thousands were slowly coalescing into their large megaships. The Navy was reacting, but for the first time, Beth wasn't sure if it was enough. Most humans had an ingrained belief in some sort of manifest destiny, and Beth was no different. It was inconceivable that they might lose this battle, but watching it unfold, she had to admit to the possibility.

"Doesn't look good, Beth," Mercy passed on the S2S. "We're getting overwhelmed."

"For now, but we've got the Tandori Line still—"

"Which is two-hundred years old and never been tested," Mercy cut in. "Not to mention the budget cuts."

Mercy was right, of course. The Home System Defense Array, better known as the Tandori Line, had been built during the Cyber Wars, to great fanfare and at great cost. It had never been used, and while it might have kept the Cyclos from attacking the home system, it had become somewhat of a political albatross, with expensive upkeep and no enemy, at least no enemy capable to taking on the heart of the Directorate.

Over the years, budget cuts had shot down a third of the "bells," as the individual projectors were called. Beth hoped that what was left would be enough, and she was sure she'd find out soon enough.

"They'll come through," Beth said, but without conviction.

"Now would be a good time to see."

Beth could agree with that. Most of the remaining bells were closer in, but Titan and Ganymede had their own bells, and there were several others spread through the outer system. Lives were being lost as the Navy attempted to blunt the attack, but the bells remained quiet.

Smaller numbers of FALs were appearing farther out, and Beth was sure that the initial calm around their little sector of space, their Kill Box, was not for long.

Sooner than expected, Beth's hunch was proven right. A flight of ninety-eight FALs jumped into the system, some two-hundred-million kiloklicks away from their position. The formation broke up, with seven heading right for SRR-1004 and Fox Flight.

"Looks like we're up," Beth passed.

Seven against four weren't terrible odds, especially with each November having five of the newest 57s. But that assumed no advances to the FAL fighters—a dangerous assumption, as Beth knew well.

She weighed her options. Her orders were brief and basic: keep SRR-1004 operational. The how was up to her.

Beth didn't even know what it did, and a cursory check revealed nothing. The specs were classified, and even if Fox Flight was tasked with defending it, she didn't have a need to know.

She assumed that it had no active defenses, at least in the military sense. It could most likely fend off scavengers, but not an enemy that only wanted to destroy it. With that in mind, she had to keep the FALs away from it, and that meant rushing to meet the oncoming enemy, not sitting back and letting them get close.

"On me in a cross-zipper. Let's go get them."

She punched in a course and started accelerating at 53 Gs, just under the limit for the Novembers before kicking G-shot. The *Tala* shot forward, her compensator fields surrounding Beth in their protective cocoon. The other three Wasps edged into their assigned position in the cross-zipper four formation.

"Deploy Snappers," she ordered.

Each November Wasp carried four of the semi-intelligent mines. If the flight failed, and the FALs kept advancing, then maybe a mine would take them out. The stealthy mines had their own propulsion system with would draw them into an oncoming FAL's path. If it got within a single kiloklick, it would detonate a single, massive pulse that should put a Crystal ship out of action.

It would be better, of course, if the SRR-1004 was protected by an entire minefield, but the home system hadn't been considered at risk. Short-sighted when the war with the FALs was already four years old. At some point, they were going to find Sol and Earth.

The *Tala's* AI would be reporting the contact up the chain, but Beth sent a message to the CO just the same, then put higher command out of her mind. Her task was now the seven FALs closing in on her and the SRR-1004 they were to protect.

Beth tagged four of the FAL's and assigned one to each of them for the first salvo of their torpedoes. But first, it was time to start degrading their shielding.

"Let's light them up. Calliope."

A "calliope" was a new technique to use against an advancing foe where each Wasp would be firing bursts from its P-18 Meson Cannon before shifting to one of the other targets. The targeting and firing were controlled by a single combat AI, in this case, the *Tala's*. The intent was to keep up a barrage of fire coming from different directions, making it more difficult for the FALs to take reactive action.

Within a few seconds, the firing controls of the other three Wasps were shunted over, and they began firing. Almost immediately, the FALs started maneuvering. Even at this short distance, it took almost ten minutes for the beam pulses to reach their targets. No one yet knew how the FALs managed their real-time detection, but physics was physics, and the speed of light still governed energy weapons.

None of the first beams hit, but they did what Beth had wanted. They disrupted the FAL formation. And with each passing second, and the two forces closed, the time between firing and hitting was getting less.

But the FALs weren't going to let Fox's firing go unanswered. They returned fire. The Navy's own quantum scanners could detect when the FALs fired, and they could give an approximate trajectory, but it wasn't exact. Beth could maneuver, losing closing speed, or continue forward and hope for the best: either a miss or that their shielding would hold.

Beth stayed their course. The P-18s were better than the older P-13s, but they were not the weapon of choice for FALs—that was their torpedoes. But they needed to close in much farther to give them a fighting chance.

With tens of thousands of FAL ships in the system, Fox Flight's mission was the seven FALs coming at them. Beth was aware of what was happening out there, but she had to push the devastation out of her mind and focus on her slice of the battle.

That was difficult, however. She didn't have eyes on individual ships, but she could see them en masse, and the naval forces around Ganymede were being pushed back. Where the hell was Big Ben, the local Tandori Line bell? It should have been deployed by now.

The *Tala's* alarm blasted through her thoughts. She'd taken a hit, knocking her shields down to 94%. At this range, with the Wasps' cloaking, it was probably more luck than anything else—the FALs knew they were there and generally where, but hopefully not their exact position—but enough bad luck on her end would splash her.

It looked like they were scoring on the FALs, however. As their distance closed, more and more of their P-18 pulses were hitting. The FAL fighters didn't falter, but at this stage of the game, attrition was still king. Degrade the shielding, knock out any systems they could, and make them more vulnerable.

"Kinda like knights jousting, huh, sista?" Mercy asked.

Beth's nerves were getting tight, the excitement kicking in as it did each time she entered into combat, but Mercy sounded calm . . . more than calm, actually, as if she didn't care.

This didn't sound like the same Mercy at whom Beth had snapped earlier.

"Mercy, are you with me?" Beth asked.

"Always with you, sista. I'm your wingman."

"That's not what I mean, and you know it. Are you mentally here?"

She could almost see Mercy shrug in that way of hers as she said, "I'm here. That's enough. And I'll try and take a fucking alien out with me. 'Sides, right now, I'm just here for the ride. This calliope is working pretty damned well, doncha think?"

Beth pulled up Mercy's bios, but there weren't any drugs coursing her body. She wasn't high. And that was almost scarier. Mercy was sure she was at the end of her run, and accepting that could be the difference between making it through the fight or not.

"Mercy Dalisay! If you think I'm just going to sit—"

Beth was cut off by more alarms. The FALs had just launched their torpedoes, a salvo of seven.

That changed things. This was early. It was the humans who usually launched first. She had her AI run the calculations; the torpedoes would impact in twelve minutes.

Once again, she had two basic choices: she could maneuver her flight, splitting them up to try and shake the oncoming torpedoes, or she could forge ahead and try to take them out.

But there really was no choice. Splitting would open the way to the SRR-1004. She had to forge ahead and shift their cannons to the torpedoes.

"I'm cutting the calliope. Control is reverting back to you. Fire your first 57 salvo and let's take out the FAL torpedoes."

Beth fired her torpedo, then locked the next one on before tagging a target, letting the others know it was hers.

Firing pulses, her P-18 was still running in the green with power and temperature. Now she was going to be drawing more juice.

The round FAL torpedoes were maneuverable, but they didn't juke like the fighters. Beth started pouring gigajoules into the torpedo while it shifted from side to side, her AI trying to calculate the greatest possibilities of a hit. And it was doing well. In the first two minutes, she had her P-18 on target for a combined twenty-one seconds. That should rise as it got closer.

And her alarms went off again. She was being hit by the FAL energy weapons. She hesitated a moment, not wanting to break lock with her target, but her shielding was being degraded with each second.

"Shit!" she yelled as she juked to break the lock on her.

Her shields had dropped to eighty-three percent. It was too early for that. She re-engaged her target torpedo, then checked the readings of the other three Wasps. All were taking damage, but Mercy, in the *Louhi*, was at sixty-three percent, by far the lowest.

"What are you doing?" Beth yelled over the net.

At that moment, Mercy's target torpedo started veering to the side.

"I'm splashing fucking alien torpedoes," she said as if lecturing a child.

She wasn't taking evasive actions, Beth knew. She was just plowing ahead.

"You can't splash torpedoes if you're dead," Beth said. "Protect yourself. That's an order!"

"Aye-aye, ma'am. Right away, ma'am."

But she was already targeting another torpedo. Beth wanted to reach across space and strangle her sister-in-law, but her own target disintegrated, and she had to shift to the next one.

The seven FAL fighters fired off another salvo, so there were now twelve torpedoes in flight, targeting the four Wasps.

And they hadn't stopped firing their energy weapons. Within limited corridors, Beth, Grape and Wingnut were weaving in and out, like children trying to avoid a sibling with a garden hose, sometimes getting splashed, most of the time clear, but each splash was cumulative. Mercy was just plowing ahead, heedless of the damage she was taking.

One, two, three more FAL torpedoes were splashed before the first salvo of human torpedoes reached the formation. The four 57s were foxes in a henhouse, jumping at the crystalline fighters. Two ran true, destroying their targets. Beth wanted to whoop, but worry for Mercy cut that immediate rush short.

And they were not out of the woods. Wingnut splashed the last incoming torpedo, but there were seven more, and these were much closer. They'd reach the Wasps in a little more than four minutes . . . which also meant the cannon fire reached the target quicker, in less than a minute.

"Third salvo, then Wingnut, Grape, get these torpedoes off our asses. Mercy, start targeting the fighters."

Mercy didn't respond, but she shifted her fire to the FAL fighters. Beth started targeting the fighters as well, pouring gigajoules after gigajoules into the enemy ships. At this range, she started getting more and more time on target, but her P-18 was heating up. She needed to start her fireturds, but doing so would pinpoint her position to the meter, rendering her cloaking useless.

She was barely aware of the first two kills, then two more torpedoes were taken out by Grape and Wingnut, one of them just a kiloklick from her. That was railgun-close, but she trusted her wingmen, and was rewarded when her P-18 burned through another fighter, bringing them down to four.

Four against four, and to her mind, that gave the advantage to the humans. One on one, the Wasps were better fighters.

"Shift tar—" she started when Wingnut's Wasp was hit by one of the incoming torpedoes.

Wingnut's bio reading flatlined.

"No!" Beth screamed, the anger building to the breaking point.

Her own bios flashed red with a request for a sedative, which Beth denied, and she fought to regain control of herself. She couldn't let anger take over.

Two FAL fighters diverted to Grape, and she rolled out of the formation to fired another torpedo, her third, then her fourth in rapid succession. She snapped back with a FAL torpedo bearing down. She fired her P-18, only to have it quit on her. It had finally overheated.

She had no choice now, and she started releasing fireturds, which were like a neon sign pointing back to her. And now she had a torpedo on her ass. Without a cannon, Beth snapped off some decoys, the same ones she'd used in the Mosquito. They wouldn't be as effective in a Wasp, especially one that was shitting out fireturds, but it was something.

The incoming torpedo was twenty seconds away, fifteen seconds away, ten seconds. Beth waited until it was five seconds before she opened up with a string of 30mm depleted uranium shells from her railgun. She thought she saw the actual explosion as at least one of the rounds hit. And she was clear.

And then there were two FALs left. Grape was maneuvering for a shot on one, and the other was pouring fire into Mercy . . .

"Hell, Mercy, break away!" she yelled over the net as she watched Mercy's shield dip below five percent.

"Love you, sista," Mercy said as her P-18, which she'd had trained on her opponent, overheated and shut down. She started to pull back, but at this range, the FAL had no problem keeping lock.

Beth fired her last torpedo, but it was too close to lock, unable to maneuver tight enough, and it shot past, missing the FAL. She tried to bring her P-18 back, but it was still down. That left one weapon, her rail gun, with half of the rounds already fired.

She was going to have one chance at this if Mercy was going to live. Beth tried to ignore the *Louhi's* shielding reading as she hesitated. Too early, and she'd miss. Too late, and Mercy would already be lost.

The *Louhi's* shielding hit one percent. It was too soon, but Beth had to act. Her targeting AI had a firing solution, but the percentage of a hit was at 15.3%. Not good enough. Beth had been in enough dogfights by now to get a feel of FAL tactics, and before even thinking it through, she manually nudged her railgun and emptied her magazine.

A railgun was accurate up to maybe a kiloklick. When she fired, the FAL was three kiloklicks away. She fired a single burst of 3247 rounds, emptying her magazine, and leading the enemy fighter at a steep angle.

The *Louhi's* shielding hit zero, and her systems went down just as the FAL fighter flew into one of the rounds and came apart.

Beth started into a tight turn to match the *Louhi's* course, then pulled out her battle display. Grape was still flying, and the final FAL was splashed.

"Angel me," she told him, knowing he'd position himself to where he could cover both Wasps.

"Mercy, you with me?"

Silence.

"Mercy!"

The *Louhi* was dead, but Mercy's bios, self-powered, showed she was alive . . . barely. Most of her body functions had ceased, but her brain, encased within her neck-cracker, was still functioning. For how long, Beth didn't know.

"What do we do now?" Grape asked.

Beth didn't have an answer. There were no more FALs in their Kill Box, nothing even close. She could tractor the *Louhi*, but go where? Closer in, the battle was raging, and the Navy was retreating.

Jump out? Join the fight?

"What the hell is that?" Grape asked in wonderment.

Beth's mouth dropped open. It was hard to tell with her quantum scanners, but something just happened, something big. She tried to get her AI to make sense of the input. It didn't do much, but just enough.

"Big Ben," she said.

Over by Ganymede, thousands of FALs had just been swept aside, and the Navy was reversing course. One, then another Tandori Line bell opened up. The battle had shifted.

Over the next two hours, Beth grappled the *Louhi*, all the while watching the battle unfold. As the data reached her normal scanners, it was becoming clear. The Navy had not been retreating. At a huge cost in lives, it had been leading the FALs into a kill zone. The ancient bells of the Tandori Line, constructed at an enormous cost and never used, had just made every uni spent worth it. They had broken the attack so completely that all that had to be done was to mop up the still huge in numbers, but now ineffective remaining FAL ships and fighters.

It would take days still, to scour the system of FALs, but the battle to save humanity was won.

NAVAL HOSPITAL, TELEX STATION

Chapter 22

"You really need to keep out of these places, sista," Beth said, taking her hand.

"At least I didn't have to G-shot," Mercy said, trying to laugh, but ending up in a coughing fit.

The autodoc beside her beeped, and something flowed down the IV and into her arm.

"Ah, that's better. All warm and fuzzy," Mercy said, slurring her words as she closed her eyes.

Beth squeezed Mercy's hand. Her friend was right, but Beth wished it had only been another G-shot. The final blast from the FAL as the *Louhi's* shield failed had broken through the protection of Mercy's neck-cracker. Her nervous system was fried.

Another few moments . . . *seconds*, the Navy surgeon had told her . . . and Mercy would be dead, just as she'd predicted.

Beth was never so glad to have Mercy be wrong.

She was alive, but hardly hale. She'd never fly again, that was for sure. The question was how much function she'd recover . . . if any. The damage to the musculature was repairable with a few grafts, even some of the major nerves. But despite the technological advances over the millennia, the human brain was still something of a mystery.

The surgeon who'd stabilized her didn't have the answers. Mercy was alive, and that was the extent to which he'd commit himself. He said that any recovery at all would be a good thing.

"I . . ." Mercy started, then trailed off.

Beth didn't know if that was the drugs or something else.

Mercy opened her eyes and saw Beth holding her hand.

"I can't feel that, you know," she said, her words quiet and hard to make out.

"It'll get better," Beth said, then hating herself for giving Mercy hope when it might not be warranted.

"It *is* better," Mercy said. "I thought . . ." She stopped a moment and took three deep breaths. "I *knew* I wasn't going to make it. I knew I was never going to see you again, see Rock again. I was never going to see Flora, yet here I am."

"Yeah, you're too ornery to die, Mercy, and you'll see Rock again." She paused, then asked, "But who's Flora?"

Mercy smiled and said, "Your niece."

"What? Is Rosalie pregnant aga—oh, hell, sista, you mean . . . ?"

A half-smile tilted one corner of Mercy's mouth, the other side slack and inert. "Yes, Cece's pregnant. With our baby. Rock's and mine."

"Why didn't you tell me?"

"I was gonna."

Beth leaned back, taking it in. She was going to be an aunt? Her cousins' kids all called her "Aunt," but this would be her first real niece.

"Satan's balls, sista," Beth said breathlessly. "I can't believe it. And if there's a silver lining to, well, you know, you'll be there now. For your daughter's birth!"

"Probably not. It's gonna take time to get back to my fighting trim, you know. But sometime. Soon, I hope."

Beth hoped so, too. But Mercy had taken a lot of damage, and she'd need operations and therapy. The Veteran's Hospital on New Cebu wasn't the most modern in the galaxy, and it was in the capital, hours away from their hometown of San Miguel.

Mercy closed her eyes, and for a moment, Beth thought she'd drifted off. Beth was about to slip out when Mercy asked, "So, what's next for you? I heard some rumors when the nurses thought I was out of it."

Beth hesitated. The survivors of the attack, along with the influx of ships and personnel from around human space, were gathering and organizing. There was no official word, but it wasn't hard to guess what was on the table.

The FALs had evidently tracked humanity when one of the six gates back in the attack on their home system hadn't been destroyed quickly enough, and a semi-sentient tracker had been attached to a fleeing Scarab. At least that was the current consensus. But in a way that still made no sense to Beth, that somehow confirmed that the FAL system was their home system.

And now, with their huge losses in the battle of Sol, the current opinion among the brass had come around to the Gospel of Admiral Gruenstein, that humanity had to attack now, before they FALs could recover, before they could grow more ships. Their homeworld had to be destroyed.

The prevailing scientific winds were that if the homeworld was destroyed, the rest of the FALs would be far less effective, maybe even rudderless. How they determined that was beyond Beth's comprehension, and she wasn't sure she bought into it. The science-types had been wrong before. Yes, individual fighters seem to lose their way when the megaships were hit, but the FALs had to have a shitload of megaships.

But even if the scientists were wrong on this, she agreed that they had to destroy their homeworld, and now, while they had to be licking their wounds.

Nothing official had trickled down to their level, but it wasn't hard to put two and two together.

There was going to be the mother of all battles, and it was going to take place in their system, not a human system. Humanity would not fail, and if the fighters and ships were lost in the attack, either by FALs or when the entire system was vaporized by their own side, well, that was an acceptable price when the rest of humanity was at stake.

It wouldn't be the entire Navy in on the attack. The civilian government had nixed that part of the admiral's plan. Some would be left behind to protect the core systems, and enough had to be to clean out the FAL tendrils that had spread throughout the galaxy.

But enough had to be committed to destroy the FAL heart, and Beth knew that what was left of the Stingers and the other squadrons with the Novembers would be on the mission.

"We don't know . . ." Beth started, but trailed off when she realized that Mercy was out.

She reached over and stroked the red hair that adorned half of her sister-in-law's scalp.

"You're going to be a good mother," she whispered before turning to leave.

"Kick some ass, sista," Mercy murmured as Beth walked out of the room.

UNKNOWN SECTOR OF SPACE

Chapter 23

"Run checks," Beth passed to Purple Flight.

The other six pilots in her flight acknowledged. Beth ran her own, watching as each one went green. The *Tala* was ready for combat.

She pulled up the others in her task-organized flight, although "task organized" was just a fancy term for "whatever they could scrape together." Only Grape and she had survived the battle from Fox Flight, and the other five pilots assigned to her had come from three different flights. Copper—Chief Petty Officer Mark de la Papas—was an experienced pilot, but none of the others had more than a year in the cockpit.

Not that she thought it mattered in the long run. They'd managed to get thirteen hours in the simulators once the mission order had been given, and even with more experienced pilots, thirteen hours was not even close to enough time to form a cohesive flight. Beth knew that this was probably going to devolve into individual fighters instead of the tight-knit team that maximized their effectiveness.

But it was what it was, and they were just going to have to make do.

"Hey, Beth," Bull broke through on the S2S.

"Hey back at you."

"You ready for this?"

"As ready as I can be. Not much time to gel, you know."

"You've got that right," Bull said. "And you've got all the boots."

"Not that it matters," Beth said. "You know what we're there for."

There was a pause, then Bull said, "We've come a long way, from . . . you know."

Yeah, I know.

"Before we shoot the gate, I know I treated you like shit when you got to the Stingers, but you're a helluva pilot, and a better wingman. I just wanted to tell you that no matter what happens today, it's been an honor."

Beth considered what he'd said for a moment. She'd long forgiven Bull for his initial treatment of her when she'd arrived in the squadron, and she'd been on good terms with him since then, but maybe she'd still held a little bit of a grudge over the last four years.

Pretty petty of me, especially considering what we're about to do.

None of that mattered anymore, and she felt something lift from her that she hadn't realized had been there.

Beth didn't have to prove herself to anyone: Bull, other pilots . . . herself. Whether it was her intuition, as Wyma contended, or pure grit and determination, she was, by any calculation, one of the best, if not the best pilot, in the Navy.

"It's been an honor to fly with you, too, Bull," she said, and, to her surprise, she meant it.

"Thanks. I'm glad to hear you say it. Well, we shoot the gate in five, so I'll see you on the flip side."

"See you, too," Beth said, knowing the chances of that were slim.

This wasn't a suicide mission, per se, at least for the Wasps. Maybe it was for the *FS Baikal*, but the Wasps, if they survived the fighting, could get back before the system was annihilated. If there was time, if the gates were still up, if a lot of things went right.

But the feeling among the pilots was that they had a mission to do, and bugging out early wasn't an option.

Beth hoped that she could get her flight back, but if she were a betting woman, she'd bet against it. The stakes for humanity were just too high.

And then it was time. The flight was aligning with the gate, in the lantern.

"You know the drill. Let's just kick some ass."

"The Swift and the Bold!" the other pilots shouted with the Stinger's new motto, and Beth felt a surge of pride. Most of them were newbie pilots, but every one of them had heart.

Two-minutes and forty-three seconds later, Purple Flight shot the gate into the Crystal home system.

THE CRYSTAL HOME SYSTEM

Chapter 24

After the initial rush, the entry into the system was almost anti-climatic. They'd been ready for bear, but the fighters and small ships entering the system were in the far reaches, out beyond the outermost planet.

The plan was to draw the FALs out, away from their home planet, an almost featureless ball fourth out from their star. In her civilian pilot days, she'd have barely given the planet a second look, but now, after multiple briefings, it was embedded into her mind. This was the home to the FALs, who lived beneath its surface. This was the hell that spawned their enemy.

Beth had expected action upon emerging from the gate, attacks by FAL pickets, their first line of defense, just like during the last battle here. Over six hundred Wasps were jumping into the system, most with a mission to engage the Crystal fighters.

But the FALs were not coming out to play. Flight after flight arrived to no opposition.

"Looks like they might be on to us," Copper passed.

"Maybe, maybe not. But it doesn't change anything. We continue on with our orders."

Purple Flight had an AOA, an Area of Operation, a dedicated spot in space, not to defend, but from which to try and egg the FALs to engage them. At their gate speed, that would take almost two hours to reach.

They could have jumped closer, of course, but they needed to give the FALs time to react. Only they weren't reacting. The system wasn't quiet. FALs were active, lots of them, but none seemed ready to take on the Wasps.

"Drop shielding to seventy-five and up your A1L-49 gain," she ordered.

This reticence wasn't like them, and Beth was afraid of an ambush. Who knew what advances they'd made with cloaking? By upping the gain on the 49, they might be able to detect FALs lying in wait for them.

But there was nothing. Their little corner of space was empty.

"Wait until the *Baikal* arrives," Copper said. "They'll react then."

Beth checked her running time. The big battle cruiser would enter the system in just over eight minutes. Manned at ten percent, it was too big of a target to ignore.

"We'll see," Beth passed back, but she had to agree with the chief. The FALs couldn't ignore it, and they couldn't let it get too close to their planet. It was powerful enough to strip the planet of life.

Not that anyone expected it to get close enough to do much to the FAL homeworld. The *Baikal* was a feint, an attempt to clear the way for the point of main effort. If all went according to plan, enough of the FALs would swarm the battleship, leaving the humans their window of opportunity for a heavily-shielded commercial sled to get close enough, and up to speed enough, to activate the system killer on board, a newly developed weapon that would vaporize the entire planet and wipe out most of the system—planets, moons, FALs . . . and, incidentally, any humans still in the fight as well.

The lesson of the last assault on the FAL homeworld had been taken to heart. Instead of three large military monitor-slash-sleds, each with a century-old planet buster, this time, a commercial barge, employing the most advanced stealth technology and running quiet, was going to try and slip in. Two monitors would escort it from a distance while the rest of the task force tried to draw the FALs away from it.

More and more Wasps arrived in the system, and so far, no fighting had broken out. Beth was no history buff, but as a student on New Cebu, she'd been taught about World War II, back on Earth during the 20th Century. Several times during the campaign for the Philippines and the rest of the Pacific, the Japanese forces had lain quiet while the Americans came ashore the scattered islands, only to unleash holy hell after the Americans were isolated from their ships.

Beth felt like an American Marine or soldier, just waiting for the inevitable Banzai charge of fanatics willing to die to save their homeland.

Who am I calling fanatics, she thought as the *Baikal* winked into the system.

There was a full admiral onboard, a Golden Tribe member at that, and a volunteer crew who would be dead soon, probably within a couple of hours, and all for the hope that their sacrifice would give the doomsday weapon a little better chance to vaporize the FAL home planet. The crew was just as fanatical as any humans in history.

On the other side of the system and below the orbital plane, one of the flights in Second Squadron finally initiated contact, jumping four FALs. It was over quickly. Using a single spread of torpedoes, they splashed the FALs within ten minutes, never having been taken under fire themselves.

Easy. Maybe too easy.

But there might be an explanation. When Commander Tuominen had taken out the FAL megaship, at the cost of his own life, the remaining FAL fighters had seemed rudderless and had been easy pickings. The xenobiologists had already determined that the FALs had something of a hive mind, interconnected, and with each individual, if you could use the term, contributing to the whole. During their mission brief, the J2 had said that it was possible that the huge loss in the human home system would have a deleterious effect on their defense.

Despite the many people clinging to that theory, Beth still thought that was too simplistic, too hopeful. This wasn't the FAL equivalent to a task force, out in the black somewhere. This was the FALs' home system, where they would have their strongest defenses. But something was up, she had to admit. The FALs were not reacting as they had in the past.

"Purple Flight, proceed to our CAP station," she passed to the other six Wasps.

It still felt weird to be using colors for the flights instead of the normal alpha-numeric terms, but it also felt weird to have seven Wasps. There were no commonly-used formations that had seven fighters. Beth had chosen to use a modified version of a Toro-yama, but with another Wasp on each end of the "horns," and the extra third back sharing the overwatch.

All around them, flights were heading to their designated CAP stations, or to be more specific in this case, their Kill Boxes, where they were to loiter on station until the FALs came out to play. Not that Beth expected to get that far. The last time she'd been in the system, the FALs had swarmed out in the thousands.

The *Baikal* was huge on her displays. She wanted to be seen, but as of yet, there was no reaction. Beth wondered how long those onboard had to live. An hour? Two hours? All of them had Beth's undying respect

Her observation that the FALs weren't reacting wasn't quite true, however. FAL craft were taking to space, but not streaming into the attack.

"They want us to press to assault them," Copper passed. "Look how they're deploying."

Beth frowned as she tried to make sense of their tactics. If they were making a defensive line, then it wasn't a very good one, in her opinion. Too many gaps.

Around them, one flight, then another engaged the FALs. No Wasps were lost. But Purple Flight arrived at the Kill Box, which was nothing more than a three-dimensional target area where no coordination was needed to engage. In other words, if anything came into their Kill Box, they were to splash it. Unless and until their box was dissolved, they were to ignore whatever was happening elsewhere. Purple Flight's mission was to draw the FALs away from the Death Barge.

And there it was. Coming into the system along with its monitors and two corvettes, it was already on its course to its target. Powered down and with the finest shielding known to humankind, Beth wasn't actually seeing the sled on her display. She was seeing an avatar created by the Coordinating AI based on its projected path. Since it was not under power, then the avatar should be an accurate indication of where it was.

The planners had expected the assault force to be engaged, so the Death Barge had come in under the cover of the two corvettes, which had now broken off and were proceeding with their mission.

"This is it, Stingers," Beth passed. "The Death Barge's on its way. One way or the other, this will all be decided within three hours."

"I still don't know why they just didn't put up a gate closer," Copper passed on the S2S.

Beth didn't know, either. Planetary gravitational pull wreaked havoc on gates, so they had to be placed away from any planetary bodies, but she had to assume a gate could be placed closer. Three hours was not a long time for intra-system travel, but when humankind depended on destroying the FAL home planet, then perspectives changed.

"We've got company," Grape said.

Keep your mind in the game, Floribeth!

He was right. A flight of what looked to be a dozen FALs seemingly dropped their cloaking and looked to be heading to them. No maneuvering, no subterfuge, but a direct approach.

"Beerman, come on up," she ordered one of her two overwatch Wasps, indicating on her HUD where she wanted him. That gave more firepower up front. "The rest of us, re-orient to the FALs."

The formation had broken their cloaking and were approaching from below the system's orbital plane, and Beth wanted to meet them head-on.

"Arm torpedoes, but don't fire until my order."

Which wasn't going to be until they entered the flight's Kill Box. The distance would still be more than two-million kiloklicks away, just over 0.01 AU, but too close for comfort when dealing with hyperspeed torpedoes and energy weapons.

Around the system, Wasps were opening up, and the *Baikal*, still hoping to get a response, was firing long-range blasts at the biggest gas giant's moon.

Everything was off, and that troubled Beth. But at the moment, she had a dozen FAL fighters heading right toward her. She had to focus on that.

"Ratchet, drop your shielding to twenty-percent and run up the gain on your SPC-33. Full coverage." she told Petty Officer Two Lara Tilton in her overwatch position. Wasp shielding sometimes caused some loss in the 33, and Beth wanted to make sure that there wasn't a cloaked FAL formation using the other FALs to focus the flight's attention.

"Roger that," Ratchet replied. Two minutes later, she said, "Lots of activity, but nothing in the Kill Box or anywhere close by."

It should have made Beth feel better, but it didn't. The FALs were always changing, innovating, but she'd seen nothing even close to this.

To Beth's surprise, a conditional recall sounded. For the bulk of the assault force, those who were not directly engaged, they were to RTB, getting out of the system before the Death Barge detonated.

"Do we RTB?" Copper asked.

Which was a good question. We're they subject to the recall? We're they even engaged? Beth watched the FAL formation as it continued to slide around Purple Flight.

"Wait one," she passed back. "Let's see how this progresses."

Which was so unlike Beth. One of her pet peeves when watching holovids was when two characters, in the middle of a fight, would freeze, their handguns pointed at the other from a half-meter away.

"Just shoot!" she'd yell, much to Mercy's delight, who would remind her this was just a holovid.

It was stupid in the holovid, and stupid here. Her flight was locked and loaded, facing an enemy who was not fighting back. She knew they could splash the entire formation, but something held her hand.

All around the system, Wasps who were not engaged were answering the recall, heading for the gates. The *Baikal*, which had destroyed the gas giant's moon, was starting back as well. It looked like their suicide mission wasn't to be.

And none of this made sense.

Beth tagged each of the remaining FALs, then assigned the targets to each pilot. If the FALs so much as blinked, Beth was going to release the flight to splash every one of them.

But still, they slowly slid around Purple Flight, taking no aggressive action.

"What are they doing?" Grape asked, breaking silence. "They just gonna dance with us or attack?"

Beth checked the time. Purple Flight had just under five minutes to spare if they were going to break contact and head back to shoot the gate before the Death Barge detonated, and that was using G-shot.

She pulled up a battle report. Close to a hundred FALs has been splashed, a moon base destroyed, and not one human had been lost.

"Commander, any word from Fleet?" she asked.

An equally perplexed-sounding XO, who was the acting commander for the operation with the CO still off flight status, said, "No one knows what's happening or why they're not engaging, but the mission stands. And you've got four minutes and twenty seconds before you have to head to your gate. Do you feel safe disengaging?"

Beth looked back at the FALs looping around her. Even after losing three fighters, they had not changed their posture.

"I think we can disengage."

"Roger that. This . . . this is not what I expected. See you in the rear, Fire Ant."

This wasn't what any of us expected.

The FALs had shown no sign of aggression, but she was sure they were not mindless, broken by the loss of their hive minds. Their patterns were too precise, especially the one doing its thing in the middle, like a . . .

Beth wracked her brain trying to remember what it reminded her of. Something, but it remained just out of reach. Something familiar, something—

"Commander! Get me a direct-connect to Wyma St. Croix. Priority One-Dash," she shouted over the S2S.

"What the hell are you talking about?" the XO answered.

"No time. But I need you to patch me through to Wyma St. Croix right now?"

"Who the hell is Wyman whoever, and what is this about?"

"Wyma St. Croix. From DAA. I don't know where she is right now, but Fleet can locate her. And I don't have time to explain. Priority One-Dash."

There was short pause while the XO considered.

"Priority One-Dash," Beth repeated.

The XO had no choice. He had to forward the call.

"God, I hope you know what you're doing," he said as he started the process. He came back twenty seconds later with "In process. Can you tell me what is going on?"

Beth started to explain but stopped. How could she say she saw a documentary on bees back at the naval hospital on Refuge, and there was a connection she couldn't quite nail down to the bees and what the FALs were doing?

"No, sir. I can't."

"You'd better be right about whatever this is, Chief Warrant Officer, or your ass is grass" he said, "Fire Ant" forgotten.

Beth almost laughed. She looked at the progress of the Death Barge. If she was wrong, her ass would be vaporized, not grass.

"Fuck, the others," she muttered.

"Purple Flight, disengage and RTB. Copper, you're in command."

"What will you be doing?" the chief asked. "Why am I in charge?"

"I'll be staying here for a while longer."

"Then we're staying, too," he said, not asking for permission but stating it as a fact.

"You don't understand. Your window to get back is rapidly closing."

"Then why are you staying, Fire Ant?" Grape asked.

"I . . . I've got something I have to do."

"For the mission?"

"Yes, I think so."

"Then we're staying with you," Copper said. "Until you leave, we stay."

"Chief, you don't understand," Beth said, pulling him up on the S2S. "If you aren't through the gate before the Death Barge detonates, you won't survive."

"Then why are you staying?"

"I have to. There's something I need to see through."

"Case closed. We'll see it through with you."

Beth swore under her breath. The man was being unreasonable.

"Look, I don't know if it's anything. But I have to try."

"Understood," he said, and left it at that.

Beth checked the time. The flight had about a minute left if they wanted to be through the gate before the scheduled detonation. It was already too late if the Death Barge had to detonate early.

"You've got forty-five seconds, Chief. Don't be a fool."

"All you reprobates," he passed, switching to the flight net. "Our fearless leader is staying put, but she wants us to leave her here. Anyone who wants to bug out for the gate, you've got thirty seconds or so. You've been ordered to do it, so no one's going to hold it against you if you go. But I'm staying."

Beth watched her display, hoping that they would leave, but they all stayed in their present formation, the FALs slowly coming around to match their course.

"Too late now, ma'am. I guess you're stuck with us," the chief said.

Beth didn't know whether to laugh or cry. She was proud of them, but she was in anguish that she may have killed them. But for what? For stray thought?

For intuition?

Wyma had told her that her intuition had kept her alive. Beth thought that this time, maybe it had killed her and her flight.

"So, do we attack the bastards?" Grape asked. "If I'm going out, I want to go out as an ace."

"Stand steady. If they attack, we'll make them pay," Beth said.

But the FALs kept to their formation, the one in the middle doing its thing, moving back and forth between the others.

More and more fighters and ships were heading to the gates. Four flights were still engaged in combat—if you could call a one-sided slaughter combat. And the Death Barge kept its course for the home planet. It was surreal.

And still, nothing from Wyma.

"Anything yet?" Beth asked the XO, her patience at an end.

"It isn't like we have a direct connection," the Lieutenant Commander Knelton snapped. "And it would help if you told me what the hell this is all about."

"I don't know," Beth said, her confidence melting like the first snow.

"You don't fucking know? You killed yourself and your flight for 'I don't know?'"

"Maybe," Beth said quietly.

"God, Dalisay. What have you done?"

Beth broke the connection.

Eight long minutes later, her earbuds activated. "Beth, is that you?"

"Wyma," she almost shouted in relief.

"What's going on? They said this is a Priority One-Dash."

"Where are you?"

"Me? I can't tell you that. Where are you?"

Screw security.

"I'm in the FALs' home system. Wherever you are, do you have a class three or better monitor?"

"What's going on, and why are you calling me?"

"Can you accept an .ffg download?"

"Uh, yeah. What do you want me to see?"

Beth hit the transmit, sending the recording of the FALs to the xenolinguist. Doing so broke every comms security procedure, but there was no time to go through proper channels.

"I've got something coming now. It looks like . . . are those . . . Crystal ships? From the battle right now?"

"Yes. I've been recording them for the last twenty minutes."

"Why is this important? What do you want me to see?"

"You told me to trust my intuition, right?"

"Well, yes," Wyma said. "And what's your intuition telling you about this?"

"Look at the one in the middle, doing its own thing."

"OK," Wyma said, said, raising the tone to make it a question.

"I think . . . it could be something. Like a bee's dance, telling the others—"

"A waggle dance. Yes, I know what that is."

There was a moment of silence, then Beth asked, "Am I crazy?"

"Can you keep streaming this?" Wyma asked with a tone of command Beth had never heard from her before.

"I think so. But I don't know for how long."

She did know, however. The Death Barge was scheduled to detonate in two hours and seventeen minutes. That was if something else didn't trigger an immediate detonation.

"I'm going to be leaving you for now. There're some things I need to check. Just keep up the stream,"

"Wyma—" Beth started, but she'd been cut off.

Beth sat there in the *Tala*, wondering if she was just being stupid . . . mortally so. Wyma hadn't reacted as Beth had expected. There was no discussion, no words of encouragement. She just cut Beth off.

She looked at the FALs again, only fifty-two kiloklicks away, more than close enough for any of their weapons. They maintained their formation, keeping their distance to the flight, but not closing.

Is there another reason for that?

Hell, I need to brief the others, she remembered, snapping her out of the whirlpool of her thoughts.

"Purple flight, we've been told to hang on."

"Do we know what's going on?" Copper asked.

"No. Not really. I'm streaming my display to Fleet now."

More and more fighters were shooting their gates, leaving the system. Beth watched the timer to the detonation click down: sixty minutes, fifty minutes, forty minutes . . .

At twenty-two minutes, fourteen seconds, the *Baikal* shot the system, the last capital ship. Thirty-nine Wasps and two Scarab shuttles remained . . . and, of course, the Death Barge and its two monitors.

At nineteen minutes, thirty-six seconds, the XO passed, "We're about to shoot our gate."

"Any word from St. Croix?"

"Wait one." A few moments later, the XO came back with, "She's not taking comms now."

Beth's heart dropped. Wyma wasn't taking a call from her? What the hell did that mean?

A sour tasted filled her mouth, and Beth whipped off her helmet, afraid she was going to puke. She put her head as far forward as she could, resting her face on her knees, as she gasped for breath.

She swallowed back down the bile, and slowly gained control of herself again. She started to put back on the helmet but then thought better of it. She let it fall to the deck of her cockpit, switching over to the *Tala's* HUD. The neck-cracker protected her brain from FAL beamers, but that didn't look to be much of a risk now, all things considered.

At eighteen minutes, ten seconds, the XO shot his gate. The entire squadron, except for Purple Flight, was safe. Eleven other Wasps were still in the system, G-shotting for their gates. Beth almost casually noted that at least six weren't going to make it, either. Purple Flight was not going to be alone.

"Ten minutes," Copper said.

Beth knew she should address them, but she didn't know if she should yell at them for being stupid or thank them for staying with her.

The FALs never wavered. They kept their distance while the one kept up its bee dance, its "waggle dance," as Wyma called it.

"Disengage lock," Beth passed as she shut down her Target Acquisition Array.

No one argued. They knew that torpedoes were OBE.

Beth was suddenly thirsty, and she took a swallow from her Number 4 nipple. Muddy Three, guaranteed to give her a lift and sharpen her thinking. It didn't do much.

Almost as an afterthought, she flipped to her Number 6, knowing that Moid wouldn't have had time to fill it, but to her surprise, a cold rush of Coke filled her mouth.

"You are the best, Moid!" she said, taking in five huge gulps. No use rationing it now.

She let out a huge burp, giving an automatic "excuse me" . . . which struck her as pretty funny. She started laughing and couldn't stop.

At three minutes, she pulled out her silver cross, letting it lie against her chest. She considered a prayer to Mother Mary, but decided against it as too self-serving.

At two minutes, while watching the FALs, Beth waggled the *Tala*, using her thrusters. She didn't know what she hoped for, but there was no reaction from the enemy fighters.

"At least you could respond," she said grumpily.

At one minute, Beth knew she had to say something, but nothing came to mind. Time was running out, so with forty seconds left to go, she went on the flight net and said, "It's been an honor."

The others chimed in, responding to her and each other in a rush, as if they'd been holding back their thoughts, and now the dam had broken.

The words petered off when the timer hit ten seconds. Beth kissed her cross, leaned her head back, and counted down out loud.

". . . seven . . . six . . . five . . . four . . . three . . . two . . . one . . . now . . . uh, one? Two . . . three?

Beth stared at the timer in a mixture of shock, relief, and hope. The time lengthening, past zero hour. The Death Barge was still on her display, still flanked by its monitors. The FALs hadn't managed to destroy it. But why hadn't it detonated?

"Um, I guess we're still here," Copper said.

The others crowded the flight net, comms discipline forgotten, and drowning each other out. Beth stayed quiet, trying to digest what was happening. Could her intuition have been right?

"What do we do now," a jubilant-sounding Copper asked her.

"Now we just wait. Someone will get back to us soon enough."

"Soon enough" was almost seven hours later, long after Beth had drained her Coke and had even hazarded eating the TN bar.

"Purple Flight, stand down," the XO passed as the official orders flashed onto her display. "Take no offensive action and RTB, I repeat, return to base."

"What's going on? Can you tell us anything?" Beth asked.

"I don't know. Whatever it is, it's way above my pay grade, but it looks like there could be a cease-fire, if you can believe that."

"A cease- fire?" Beth asked in wonder.

"I don't know what the hell you told that scientist, but it sure has had a major impact on everything. Everyone's going batshit crazy." There was a pause, then, "I'm out of the loop, but I've got to know. What did you tell your scientist?"

"I really didn't tell her anything. I just told her to look at my feed of the FALs."

"You sent a battle feed to a civilian? Why in the name of all that's holy did you do that?" the XO asked.

"Intuition."

NEW CEBU

Epilogue
Two years later . . .

"Ma'am? Are you the Fire Ant?" the young girl asked.

Beth looked up from her pad and sat up straighter, pulling down on the bottom of her Charlies' jacket.

The girl, no more than ten, had that hero-worshipping glint in her eyes, but tinged with obvious nervousness. She waited breathlessly for Beth to respond.

Beth had hoped to slip home unnoticed, but humanity was still technically at war, so all travel was to be done in uniform. With her Dress Charlies, with ribbons and pilot's wings, it was probably a little much to hope for.

"Yes, I'm Ensign Dalisay. Fire Ant's my call sign."

A smile almost split the girl's face in two, and she turned around to say to an older women, who was trying to act like she wasn't paying attention, "It is her! You were right!

"I want to be just like you, one day," she said, spitting the words out like the *Tala*'s railgun. "I want to be a Wasp pilot!"

"What's your name?" Beth asked.

"Gladiola Salcedo, but my friends call me Glad, ma'am."

"If you want to be a pilot, Glad, then don't let anything get in your way."

The girl nodded and said, "I won't. I promise."

Beth reached into her jacket pocket and pulled out a challenge coin, her personal one with an image of the *Tala* and the word "Stingers" on one side, her name and rank over the Navy logo on the other. She'd had one made in .99 silver to give to Petty Officer Grylmor for that first salute she'd received as a warrant officer, what seemed like decades ago. It had taken her a year to get it to him, but better late than never.

His reaction to receiving it was surprising, and his gratitude had given her pause. So, she'd had another two-hundred made—these only clad in silver—to give out when she thought it appropriate. And this seemed like one of those times.

"Here, take this, Glad. When school gets tough, when you get frustrated, you take it out to remind you of your goal. OK?"

Gladiola's mouth dropped open as she looked at the coin in her hand.

"I don't . . . I . . . thank you!" the girl said, her voice choking up. "I won't forget!"

"We are about to begin our descent to White Mountain Spaceport," came over the speakers. "Please take your seat and fasten your safety belts."

The girl looked at Beth wide-eyed as she clutched the coin in a death grip, then to Beth's surprise, she leaned forward and hugged her. Beth hadn't expected that, but she put a tentative arm around the girl and gave a gentle squeeze back.

The girl broke free and ran to her seat, where her mother mouthed a "thank you" to Beth.

"You'd better get used to it," the older gentleman said from the seat beside her.

"Sir?"

"You need to get used to it, Ensign Dalisay. You're more than a hero to all of us Cebuanos."

Beth furrowed her brow. She knew she was somewhat of a celebrity. A minor one, to be sure, but still known, and even those civilians who didn't know her might recognize the Order of Honor on her chest. But for the last two years, she'd been surrounded by her fellow sailors. This was her first leave since the war paused, the first time back home.

"I wasn't expecting that," she said quietly.

"You made us all proud, ma'am."

"Please, I'm just Beth. Not ma'am," she said, embarrassed that the grandfatherly-looking man was deferring to her.

"Sorry, but no, ma'am. Petty Officer Third Class Henry Darroca, too many years ago. I may be old, and I may not have been in for a career, but I still know how to address an ensign."

The shuttle pulled out of the liner that had brought Beth home, and Beth leaned back in her seat. The gentleman went back to his pad, leaving Beth to her thoughts for the forty-five-minute flight down to the spaceport.

The last two years had been non-stop. The ceasefire was holding while Wyma and the others headed the negotiations with the FALs . . . *Crystals*, that is (the government didn't want them to be called "Fucking Aliens" anymore).

Negotiations.

That still felt weird to Beth. How does someone negotiate with a lifeform where there was no common ground? Beth's intuition, in this case, had been proven right, for as far as it went. The Crystal fighter's vibrating waggle dance was an attempt to communicate, being repeated all over their home system and scattered around the galaxy. In almost every case, either the dance was to unarmed commercial vessels or to Navy ships that immediately attacked and destroyed the messengers.

It took Beth, even if she didn't really understand what was happening, and Wyma, who was one of the few humans alive who could have quickly made the connection, to realize what the Crystals were attempting to do. There was no doubt that the analysts and AIs would have made more sense of it after the fact . . . and after the home system had been destroyed.

But then what? Try to clean up every Crystal infestation in the galaxy? And as humans now knew, the "cutting off the head" would only affect a portion of the "resonance mind," as it was now called. Beth thought of it as a tribe losing its chief, but the other tribes being able to carry on.

Beth had felt abandoned after she started streaming her feed, but Wyma had been running analysis while fighting at the government's highest levels at the same time. Most of the decision-makers wanted to continue the attack, to destroy the system. If they acknowledged the fact that the Crystals could be trying to communicate, then that was a sign of weakness, one that must be exploited.

But cooler heads prevailed. Despite not knowing for sure if it even was an attempt at communication, thirteen minutes and four seconds before detonation, the Death Barge was reprogrammed to move into orbit around the Crystals' home planet, still armed and ready to detonate.

Then the real work had begun. Cracking the code had proven to be much more difficult to accomplish, even with immense resources being thrown at it. Wyma, who'd been the tip of the spear, was far too junior to be in the leadership of the effort, but she was still part of the team.

Part of the team, but mostly out of Beth's life. They'd managed to talk twice, but their paths had diverged. Wyma was trying to establish communications, while Beth was trying to rebuild the ravaged fleet.

The Navy had lost eighteen percent of its capital ships during the first attack on the Crystals' home system, and then during their attack on Sol. But the loss of fighters had been sixty-seven percent.

The Navy left all the attempts at diplomacy to the civilians and put all its efforts into rebuilding the fleets. The ceasefire was holding, but for how long?

Beth was awarded the Distinguished Achievement Medal, something normally awarded to captains and admirals, for her part in the fight. Then, as the Navy's top living ace again—Killjoy Reicher had more kills before he was lost in the Battle of the Home System—she left the Stingers to spend eighteen months at flight school, pushing candidates through the pipeline. Maybe the brass thought some of whatever she had, skill or intuition, would rub off on the new pilots. It might have been necessary, but it was boring, and Beth couldn't wait to leave.

Then she had her chance to cut that tour in half. She'd been offered a line commission and a jump to ensign, and after more than a little consideration, she accepted. Six weeks of OCS with the other warrants and enlisted getting commissioned, then with her shiny new gold bars, it was back in a Wasp, on picket duty on the outskirts of the "Crystal One," the Navy's term for the Crystals' home system . . . and if anything, it had been even more boring than flight school. Eight hours in the cockpit flying spherical holes in the black, then twelve hours off, day in, day out. And without Moid, no Coke to break the monotony.

And now, before reporting to her new squadron, she had three weeks of leave. She looked at the visual repeater as the shuttle descended toward the planet's surface.

Home.

Not the most beautiful planet in the galaxy with the browns and tans, but it made her heart sing.

The last time she was home was for Mercy's wedding, where she'd been interrupted by her dogfight to save the planet. The quick recollection made Beth gulp. That fight hadn't been intuition. She'd had no idea that they would be attacking New Cebu. It had been pure, unmitigated luck that she was in the right place at the right time.

Because of that attack, however, she could never really trust the Crystals. They tried to kill all who she loved. If rumor was right, there was an agreement being formed that would divvy up parts of the galaxy. Crystals and humans evidently had different concepts on what constituted a livable planet, which made sense given their entirely different biological make-up. It might be logical to allow the Crystals to take planets where they could live while they ceded Earth-like planets to the humans.

But Beth still didn't trust them, and if they were allowed to settle Mayari, the sixth planet in the New Cebu system, well . . .

The shuttle started its final approach, pulling Beth out of her thoughts. The closer the shuttle approached, the more excited she got. She was finally going to see her family. And food! Filipino food that wasn't dialed up on some generic fabricator.

Sisig! she almost shouted out loud, her mouth watering at the thought.

Her extended family was arranging a fiesta in San Miguel, but before anything else, she wanted to sink her teeth into her ina's sisig.

The autopilot brought the shuttle to a gentle landing, and maybe a third of people clapped and cheered. Probably Off-Planet Workers, coming home after long stints away. Beth grabbed her go-bag and joined the line to debark. A middle-aged man ahead of her leisurely stood, started talking to the young woman who'd been sitting next to him, and slowly took his carry-on from the bin. Beth wanted to scream at him to stop hitting on the woman and get his butt off the shuttle.

In her frustration, she looked to her right where little Gladiola was watching to catch her eye. The girl smiled and held up the challenge coin. Beth smiled back, and she suddenly felt better. Anxious to see her family, but not as antsy. She still didn't understand why people took so long to debark a shuttle, but she could handle it.

Finally, though, she made it off and to arrivals. While in uniform, Beth could use the official business line, and she was going to use the privilege.

"Welcome home, Ensign Dalisay," the agent said, before she'd even scanned her eyes.

I guess the old petty officer was right, she thought as she smiled and thanked the man.

Hopefully, things would be better in San Miguel. The people there had known her since she'd been a baby, after all.

The scan took all of five seconds, and she was waved through. She had no luggage (this was only three weeks, and if the things in her go-bag weren't enough, she could always bum some clean clothes from her mom), so it was straight out and into the arrival lounge.

Several people started snapping holos of her, and a reporter Beth didn't recognize immediately turned to her holographer to start some sort of introduction, but Beth had only eyes for the group standing quietly to the left.

She ignored the questions and welcomes coming her way and made a beeline for her family: her mother, looking reserved, but a tear beginning to form in the corner of her eye; Cece, already showing; Rock, his hand on his wife's shoulder; Mercy, in her medchair; and sitting on her lap . . .

"Is that Floribeth?" she asked, coming to a stop just short of her family.

"I sure hope it is, sista," Mercy said. "Otherwise, we've spent a lot of time raising someone else's kid."

"Can I . . ." she started, holding her hands out.

Little Floribeth looked at Beth with uncertain eyes, not sure who this strange woman was.

"Take her. She's not going to break. Rock . . ."

Rock stepped around his wife and picked up Floribeth, who wrapped her arms around his neck in a death grip.

Beth took a step forward to take her, but the little girl was having none of it. She gave a squawk and turned her face away.

Everyone laughed, but Beth felt hurt. This was her namesake, and she wanted the girl to love her.

"Don't worry. She'll get used to you. She's just a little fussy, especially with the crazies getting in our faces."

As if on cue, the reporter rushed forward. "Ensign Dalisay! Irene Viogele, NCB News. Can I talk to you for a moment?"

A spaceport security guard moved forward and got between them.

"It's been like this since we got here. What did the Navy do? Call them for publicity?" Mercy asked.

"I'm old news," Beth said.

"Not here," Rock added as Floribeth turned around to regard Beth.

"And this is little Grey," Mercy said, reaching out a shaky hand to pat Cece's belly.

"Cece! So good to see you," Beth said, reaching over to hug her cousin.

Her belly, with Mercy and Rock's son, bumped up against Beth's.

Beth turned around and asked, "Grey? As in the CO?"

Mercy nodded and said, "Without him snagging you, none of this would never have happened. And then, during the fight with the megaship, you know . . ."

Yeah, we'd both be dead.

It was a fitting name.

Beth started to give Rock a hug, but Floribeth flinched, and she turned it into a sisterly pat on the arm. Turning to her mother, she almost folded into her arms, the little girl come home.

"Welcome home, Floribeth," her ina whispered into her ears.

"I am so glad to be here," she said, all the stress of the last few years melting away. That's the power of a mother.

Beth's tears dropped on her ina's shoulder, and with an embarrassed laugh, Beth pulled back and wiped her eyes. Most of the people around them were watching, some taking snapshots. The reporter was anxiously waiting, looing over the security guard's shoulder.

Mercy raised her good hand and touched Beth's arm. "It's good to see you, sista."

Beth gave the hand a squeeze. "How're you doing? I mean, you know."

"You're asking if I'm ever going to get out of this robochair? I don't know."

"She's making progress," Rock said. "Lots of it."

"If you mean I can wipe my own ass now, then sure," she said, waving her good arm.

"Ass!" Floribeth repeated, clear as day.

"Mercy!" Beth's mother admonished.

"She's trying to clean up my language," Mercy said, "now that I'm a mom."

Rock just rolled his eyes while Cece laughed aloud.

"Ensign! Can I have a few minutes of your time?" the reported yelled out.

Beth looked for an escape route. "Can we just go home? I can't wait to see everyone."

"Uh, about that," Rock said. "Change of plans. We've got rooms at the Dusit Thani for the night."

"But, the fiesta? And it's still morning here!" Beth said, almost whining.

"The governor wants to have a dinner. Not a huge function," Rock quickly added when Beth started to protest. "Just a private dinner with his family and some students from different schools. He's got an initiative that he wants to discuss with you."

Beth looked to her mother for support, but she said, "I think we need to do it, Floribeth. Think of the good it will do."

"But I'm just a Wasp pilot," Beth said.

"Right, sista," Mercy said with a snort. "Who saved this planet, among everything else. You made your bed, and now you've got to lay in it."

Beth looked at the people gathered. The ones near her were openly listening for what she was going to say.

Mercy was right, she knew, as much as she just wanted to be a regular person.

No, that wasn't right. She didn't want to be "regular." She wanted to be special, to be the best. She might not be the Navy's top ace anymore, but she sure had blazed a trail that no one could match.

All these people watching her, they were alive because of her. And if that meant she couldn't come home anonymously, then the price was worth it. It wasn't even a question.

And if this was the bed she made, as Mercy said, she might as well embrace it, to do what good she could for as long as she had a pulpit.

"I'll give you four minutes," she called out to the reporter. "Just give me a sec.

"Let me get this over with, then we can go to the hotel. I need to get out of this uniform and get it cleaned if we're having a dinner tonight," she told her family. "And I want all the gossip from home. Everything."

"I've got you covered for that," Cece said, her eyes lighting up.

"Maybe we can get some Jollibee's for lunch, at least." She gave a sigh. "I was so looking forward to the fiesta today. My mouth was watering on the way down."

Rock looked to their mother, who now had a self-serving smile. She reached into her bag and brought out a cyropack, which she handed to Beth.

Beth cracked open the tab, and a heavenly aroma hit her.

"It's your sisig!" she exclaimed excitedly.

"You may be a hero and all of that, but you're still my daughter, and I'll always be here to take care of you."

Thank you for reading *Indomitable*. I hope you enjoyed this book, and I welcome a review on Amazon, Goodreads, or any other outlet.

If you would like updates on new books releases, news, or special offers, please consider signing up for my mailing list. Your email will not be sold, rented, or in any other way disseminated. If you are interested, please sign up at the link below:

http://eepurl.com/bnFSHH

OTHER BOOKS BY JONATHAN BRAZEE

The Navy of Humankind: Wasp Squadron
Fire Ant
Crystals
Ace
Indomitable

The United Federation Marine Corps
Recruit
Sergeant
Lieutenant
Captain
Major
Lieutenant Colonel
Colonel
Commandant

Rebel
(Set in the UFMC universe.)

Behind Enemy Lines
(A UFMC Prequel)

The Accidental War (A Ryck Lysander Short Story Published in *BOB's Bar: Tales from the Multiverse*)

The United Federation Marine Corps' Lysander Twins
Legacy Marines
Esther's Story: Recon Marine
Noah's Story: Marine Tanker
Esther's Story: Special Duty
Blood United

Coda

Women of the United Federation Marine Corps
Gladiator
Sniper
Corpsman

High Value Target (A Gracie Medicine Crow Short Story)
BOLO Mission (A Gracie Medicine Crow Short Story)
Weaponized Math (A Gracie Medicine Crow Novelette,
Published in *The Expanding Universe 3. Nebula Award Finalist*)

The United Federation Marine Corps' Grub Wars
Alliance
The Price of Honor
Division of Power

Ghost Marines
Integration
Unification
Fusion

The Return of the Marines Trilogy
The Few
The Proud
The Marines

The Al Anbar Chronicles: First Marine Expeditionary Force--Iraq
Prisoner of Fallujah
Combat Corpsman

Sniper

Call to Arms: Capernica
Conscientious Objector
POG
Veteran

Werewolf of Marines
Werewolf of Marines: Semper Lycanus
Werewolf of Marines: Patria Lycanus
Werewolf of Marines: Pax Lycanus

Soldier

Animal Soldier: Hannibal

To the Shores of Tripoli

Wererat

Darwin's Quest: The Search for the Ultimate Survivor

Gemini Twins

Venus: A Paleolithic Short Story

Secession

Duty

Semper Fidelis

Checkmate (Originally Published in The Expanding Universe 4)

Golden Ticket

With Time All Things Revealed

The BOHICA Chronicles (with Michael Anderle and C. J. Fawcett)
Reprobates
Degenerates
Redeemables
Thor

Seeds of War (With Lawrence Schoen
Invasion
Scorched Earth
Bitter Harvest

Non-Fiction

Exercise for a Longer Life

The Effects of Environmental Activism on the Yellowfin Tuna Industry

Author Website

http://www.jonathanbrazee.com

Twitter

https://twitter.com/jonathanbrazee